INFIN

Book Three in the
'Curator Angelus' Trilogy

To my husband, Richard, who continues to support
and encourage me.

Chapter One

Hide And Seek

After falling asleep at her sister's funeral, Lisa Brook experienced an out-of-body experience. From the corner of her mother's kitchen ceiling, she had hovered and witnessed the maid shout and make a grab for her son. Unaware of the outcome because she had woken, she dashed from the chapel to her car.

The dress code at Susan Jones's funeral had been casual. Lisa had worn her usual attire: jeans and a T-shirt. However, if she were given the choice to attend again, she would decline without hesitation because her family were rude to her at the service. They had alienated her, so she was seated alone on a back pew.

Her car was parked on a side road where there were six large, detached houses down one side and woodland on the other. Her car was blocked in. A convertible was parked behind, and an SUV was in front.

She twisted her fingers through her hair while she stamped her feet. 'I don't *effing* believe this,' she grumbled.

She wore a pair of tatty old trainers, which were comfortable as they had stretched in the right places, but every time she stamped her right foot, a stone, which had lodged in the sole, gradually pushed through until it jabbed her foot. She pulled it out and tossed it into the trees. With her arms down by her sides, she stood still, took deep breaths, balled her hands into fists and dug her nails into her palms.

'Why do some people have to park so *effing* close?' She looked up at the sky and put her palms together to pray. 'I need to get back to my little boy. He might be in danger.' She stepped back to gauge how wide the gaps were between the cars. 'Bumper to bumper.' She shook her head. 'Why? I'm sure some people like to park like this on purpose. Look at all the space there is as well.' She gestured. 'It's not like this road's full of parked cars.' There were only three cars on the entire road. 'I bet the owners aren't around either.' She checked along the road in both directions. She was right. No one was in sight. 'I haven't got time to hang around. It might be quicker if I run back to get Peter and then come back later to collect my car.'

After a moment's consideration, she unlocked the car and got in. She looked at herself in the rear-view mirror, smirked and then nodded. She turned the key in the ignition. The engine did not start. All the symbols on the dashboard lit up. Her car had never let her down before. She counted to ten, emphasised the word *please* between each number and then turned the key again. The engine started. 'Thank God.' She tried to put the car into reverse, but the gearstick was stuck. It felt like someone, or something stopped her. She tried again with both hands. The gearstick slotted into position. 'Sorry.' She released the handbrake and, out of habit, looked in the rear-view mirror. 'You've been a loyal friend, but needs must and all that.' The tyres screeched. 'I hope I don't cause you too much damage.'

The convertible's alarm sounded louder than she expected as she crashed into its bumper. 'Oops.' She chuckled. 'I hope you're insured, loser.' But there was no one there to listen or to see her erratic behaviour. 'Maybe next time you'll think about parking with a bit more consideration,' she shouted.

But when she checked, she had only nudged the car. 'Oh no, I'll have to do that again.' She looked at herself in the mirror and shrugged. 'Now isn't that a shame?'

The underside of her foot throbbed and her palms smarted. She wiggled her toes and examined the nicks on her palms where her nails had dug in. There was a small amount of blood. She wiped it on her jeans. She rubbed her hands together and tried to change into first gear. Again, the gearstick proved awkward, and she had to use both hands.

With her hands positioned at ten to two, she kept the steering wheel level and ploughed forward. Her body jerked as she crashed into the SUV. Its alarm synchronised with its flashing lights. 'Wow.' Her eyes lit up. 'What a buzz. This is fun.' Her smile disappeared. She shook her head. *What am I doing? Stop messing about and get back to Peter.*

She turned on the car stereo. A tune she had never heard before played on a local radio station. The music sounded too up to date for her; although, the tune was catchy, and the rhythm also synchronised with the flashing lights and alarms. She turned up the

3

volume to try to drown out the background noises, manoeuvred forwards and backwards, several more times, before she pulled out and got on her way.

*

Eliza had only taken her eyes off Peter for a second, to look out of the window, and when she looked again, he was gone.

Bedraggled, she searched the kitchen. 'Where are you?' she taunted. She stopped to massage her ankle.

Days earlier she had offered to look after him, so Lisa could attend the funeral. Would it have been good for his well-being to watch the grown-ups as they cried and swapped, good and bad, memories? The family had agreed after a show of hands. A decision was made – he was too young to learn about death and should be protected for as long as possible. Lisa was outvoted.

Without protest, Lisa had failed to mention that she already knew he had seen his Auntie Susan's corpse on the lake.

Eliza thought he had been playing hide and seek. When the two of them had played the game before, she always pretended she could not find him. He always jumped out or gave away where he was hidden because he shouted, 'Come and find me.'

However, he was not playing, did not want to play at anything anymore and not with her. Yes, he was hidden, but it was doubtful she would seek him.

He had not been under her feet. He had played underneath the kitchen table with his toy cars and had not thought his sound effects annoyed her. As far as he knew, he had not been naughty. She had stormed in, red-faced, and shouted something, perhaps even someone else's name. Her words sounded neither coherent nor English. She hurried forward and grabbed him. Her hands surrounded the tops of his arms. He did not cry despite his discomfort.

Unbeknown to her, five small black shadows stirred behind her.

He knew they were there, but he did not look at them or warn her. Instead, he had tried to wriggle from her grip and kicked her ankle.

She released him, lost her balance, but did not fall.

What else was he supposed to do? He was fed up with grown-ups who wanted to hurt him. He needed Mummy to hurry back from the funeral, so he could tell her what Eliza had done. Mummy always knew what to do.

Before his auntie had died, she had been horrible to him, and now Eliza behaved in the same way. Before, she had always been nice. She sneaked goodies from the kitchen: a bun or a biscuit, fresh from the oven, wrapped in a sheet of kitchen roll. 'Shush, it's our little secret,' she always said as she put her index finger to her pursed lips and winked. 'But be careful, Peter, it'll still be hot. Remember to blow. We don't want you to burn your mouth.'

Not wanting to give away her location or give him a chance to work out what her next move might be, she took off her shoes and placed them on the floor. She knew all his usual hiding places and wanted to surprise him; although, it would only be a matter of time until he gave himself away.

She tiptoed into the living room and peeked behind the furniture; even in places where it was obvious, he would not fit. She checked behind opened doors and inside cupboards where he might have been able to squeeze into. As she moved from room to room, her patience dwindled. Her footsteps became heavier. There was a trail of evidence with upturned furniture and cupboard doors left open.

He was hidden well, in a new place, where she would never think to look; however, not one he had chosen.

She stopped in the master bedroom, scratched her head and pondered where she might have hidden if she were little again, but voices interrupted her thoughts. There were some pleasant words of reassurance amongst the remarks with evil intent. She pressed her hands against her ears, but the voices continued.

An unexplainable anger overwhelmed her. Within seconds, she screamed like a banshee. With her hands balled into fists, she tapped her knuckles against her temples and then slapped her forehead several times. Her anger only subsided when she punched a partition wall. *What's wrong with me? Why can't I think straight? Why do I feel so angry?* She scanned the room. There was no one there. *And where are those voices coming from?* She looked at the wall, with her fist still inside, and pulled out her arm. Debris fell on to the carpet. She checked her knuckles.

A cupboard door slammed shut. She kept still and tried to work out where the noise had come from. Blood dripped on to the cream carpet from a wound under her little finger.

As she tiptoed towards the door, she adorned the carpet with a trail of red dots. She stopped in the doorway, placed her injured hand against the doorframe and looked out along the landing. There was no one there. She heard the same voices again, behind her: 'That noise came from the kitchen. Peter must be hiding in there. Go and teach the boy right from wrong. He needs discipline in his life.'

'Leave the boy alone. He is only a child for Heaven's sake. You have already scared him half to death.' The voice chuckled.

As she turned round to check, she knew no one would be there. She started to question if the voices were inside her head and if she should listen to them.

A kitchen chair scraped along the floor. Even though the sound only lasted a couple of seconds, it echoed through the house and made her teeth grind. With her arms poised mid-air, she was about to cover her ears again, but the voices made her hesitate: 'See, I *told* you he is in the kitchen.'

'He thinks it is safe to come out. He will be playing with those matchbox cars or with something equally annoying. He will be doing those ridiculous siren imitations again.'

'What if he is? What else is there for a little boy to do? He is not doing any harm. Leave him alone. Let the boy be a boy.' The voice chuckled.

'But he is *not* just a boy, is he? We know what he *really* is.'

The voices stopped. She lowered her arms and checked around. Mindful the voices might start again, she listened intently. The house was still again, yet the hairs on her arms stood on end.

As she went down the stairs, she wondered if the sounds from the slammed cupboard door and the chair, which had scraped along the floor, were made by Peter. Perhaps Mr and Mrs Caplin or Lisa had returned home, or maybe an intruder had somehow got in. *Did I lock the doors?*

The stairs carpet felt soft like cotton wool. She knew where to tread so the wood did not creak. With every step, the atmosphere grew heavier like she waded through water with a strong undercurrent. Her heart rate quickened; she heard every beat as if she listened through a stethoscope.

When she reached the bottom, she stopped. Hesitant to go further, she looked across at one of the toppled sofas. *Did I do that?* Her memory was hazy. She noticed eight zipped compartments of the same size on the underside. *So, that's one of the places where Mr Caplin hides his drugs.* She nodded. *A little obvious, yet genius. I bet the other sofa's full, as well. I wonder where the other storage areas are. The outhouses are too obvious, but then so are the sofas.*

Her curiosity got the better of her. *I'll take a little peek. I'm not harming anyone, am I? No one will ever know.* She made her way towards the sofa. The sofa started to shake, but it did not deter her as she wanted to investigate what was hidden inside before she put it upright again.

The voices started again and made her jump: 'Do not be foolish, Eliza. Put the furniture straight, tidy-up and pretend you did not see anything.'

'What if Mr Caplin were to come back early and catch you in the act? You are aware of what he would do to you. You have heard the rumours, like most people in the village.'

'Go on, be a devil. You know you are going to look anyway. There is no one here; although, I would be quick in case someone comes home.'

The voices stopped. She reached for one of the zips, but with her arm still poised mid-air, she had to step back when the sofa shook again. *Am I going mad?* She took another step back and watched the sofa as it tried to put itself upright. *Oh no!* Her eyes widened. *I hope Peter wasn't behind the sofa when it fell. Is he trying to lift it?* She furrowed her brow. *No, don't be silly, it can't be him, he's not strong enough.*

With her mouth open, she watched until the sofa was upright. Its front feet hit the floor with a thud. *What's happening? What did I just witness?* With stiffened shoulders and clasped hands, she made her way to check behind the sofa. She needed to know if he was there; although, it took her a moment to pick up the courage to look down at the floor. Relieved, she sat down on the back of the sofa and tried to figure out how it had moved.

Another kitchen cupboard door slammed shut. She jumped. 'Peter, is that you?' She made her way towards the kitchen. 'You're not in any trouble.'

The voices reappeared: 'Where do you think you are going, Eliza?'

'Are you insane? You have no idea what is in there or what is going on.'

'Grab your belongings and escape this crazy place before something bad happens to you.'

The voices stopped.

'Where are you, Peter?' She no longer taunted him. 'I promise I'm not cross. I'm sorry if I frightened you before. I don't know what came over me. I don't know about you, but I don't want to play this game anymore. You win.'

Chapter Two

The Dog Walker

A vibrant rainbow caught Lisa's attention, in her mirrors, as she manoeuvred around the potholes. Sunlight reflected off the road and made visibility difficult. A couple of the smaller potholes caught her off guard and felt deeper than they looked; her suspension took the brunt. One of the potholes, that she managed to avoid, was so big she thought it might develop into a sinkhole and swallow her and her car whole.

She had checked for closed-circuit television cameras on the lampposts and outside each house. *I thought at least one of these houses might've had a camera. If I owned one of these, I'd have some type of security.* She thought it strange how no one had investigated where the noise came from.

She braked at the end of the road. Her car felt different and did not drive the same. *Maybe I'll take Robert up on his offer and let him buy me a new car.* The main road was quiet. Out of habit, she still looked both ways. Unaware she had a broken light, she signalled left.

A police siren sounded out in the distance. Unsure of how far away the police car was, she started to feel apprehensive. *I need to get away from here before they catch up with me. If they see the state of my car, they'll know I'm the one who smashed into those two cars. They'll waste my time with one of them breathalyser tests and ask me a load of inane questions. There's something much more important I need to be*

11

doing. If I tried to explain my circumstances to them, they wouldn't listen or even try to understand.

The siren drew closer.

To her right, a long empty paved driveway ran down the side of a detached house. Its large wrought-iron gate was open. She deliberated: *If I drive off now, it'll be my luck those officers pass me. It'd probably be safer if I park on that driveway until the coast's clear.* She gave the idea no further consideration, manoeuvred, and tried to look inconspicuous.

But what if the police come down this road? They're bound to see me. Should I abandon my car and make my way back on-foot? In hindsight, that's what I should've done in the first place. I could come back later and collect my car before whoever lives here gets back from work. With a bit of luck, they work long hours, and they'll never know I was here. And it looks like the neighbours aren't at home to tell them either.

Two Alsatians lived at that house. They were at home. They had heard her car pull up and leapt on to the snuggle chair under the window. Their front paws rested on the sill. Their snouts pressed against the window. They snarled and stared at her. Strands of thick saliva trickled down the steamed-up pane.

Unaware of the dogs, she contemplated her next move. There was still not a soul in sight or a neighbour checking on where the noise might be coming from. *I wonder what the people who live on this road do for a living. I bet they're doctors, dentists, or professors.*

Someone's watching me. She turned her head to check, saw the dogs, scowled at them, displayed her teeth, and then growled.

The dogs stopped for a moment, stared, and then started to howl.

A police car sped past the end of the road. They did not appear to be interested in the noise from the cars' alarms. *They don't even know what I've done. Hang on. They might realise they've missed the turning and backtrack.* She waited a moment to make sure, but the siren became more distant. *Maybe they're on their way to an accident and that's why the roads are so quiet.*

She turned off the radio, got out of her car and left the door open. Her arms swung backwards and forwards as she skipped towards the house. Like a five-year-old in the school playground, her head lolled from side to side.

Eager to get to her, the dogs headbutted and clawed at the glass.

Her skip changed into a walk as she made her way along the lawn in front of the house. As she got closer, she noticed the dogs were young. She also knew they would love to dig their canines into her flesh. *Which part of me would they bite first? Would they prefer a limb, or would they go straight for my jugular?* She would try to be gentle with them.

She stopped in front of them and turned to stare into the eyes of what she believed was the alpha: bigger and positioned higher. *Challenge the leader and the other will submit.*

The alpha snarled briefly and then whimpered. It was easier than she thought. She expected the other dog to react in the same way. And it did, only quicker.

Both dogs lowered their heads as if chastised, jumped down and scurried away.

As she made her way back towards her car, she noticed the damage. She crouched at the rear to get a better look before she made her way to the front. Her lights were smashed, and she would need new bumpers. *Ah well.* She shrugged. *It's only a car. A good car, but still … only a car. At least it's still driveable.* She got in, shut the door, pulled her seatbelt across, and looked across at the living room window. The dogs had not returned.

A tall broad-shouldered man, with a small dog under his arm, appeared from the woods.

About to pull out of the drive, she looked across at him. *That's a little dog for a big man. I wonder if that Chihuahua belongs to his wife or his mum.*

He made his way towards the two parked cars.

Does one of those cars belong to him or is he being nosy? He acted calm, so she presumed the latter. *If someone had smashed into my car their head would roll.* She checked both ways, turned right and stopped at the junction. The main road was still quiet. She was about to pull out when she noticed the dog walker in her rear-view mirror. He waved his arms around and shouted in her direction. She could not hear him but imagined the words he used. She pulled out to her left.

Approximately one hundred yards later, she had to stop at a pelican crossing. There were no pedestrians in sight. 'Okay, which idiot pressed the button?' She had wanted to wind down her window and shout but thought better of it. *It was probably only a child and now they're hiding.*

The red light remained. Her patience dwindled. 'Come on. Hurry up.' She tapped her fingers on the steering wheel. *Why's it taking so long? These lights must be broken.* She sighed and checked above the lights for a sensor or CCTV. There was neither. *Should I drive through?* The dog walker appeared in her rear-view mirror again.

With his mobile phone held up in front of him, he made his way towards her, in the middle of the road, and took a photograph of her car.

Her attention wavered between him and the red light. Already in first gear with handbrake off, she was ready to go.

He stopped, rang someone, and then continued towards her.

She did not have time for confrontation and decided to jump the light. What did it matter? She was already in trouble. *It'll take the police a while to track me down from the photo on that dog walker's mobile phone; my car is still registered to my old address. Anyway, with a bit of luck, I'll get back before they manage to catch up with me.* She checked her mirrors. The dog walker appeared in all of them. He jumped up and down in the middle of the road. She could not see his facial expression but knew it would be one of frustration. He reminded her of a cartoon she used to watch where one of the characters had a huge spring instead of legs.

On the path, on the other side of the road, two women jogged towards her. Squeezed into vibrant coloured spandex outfits, both wore make-up as though they had not expected to work up a sweat. Their ponytails swayed like they swatted away troublesome flies. Were they on their way to audition for roles in The Real Housewives of Cumbria? Lisa recalled a poster in the post office window. They gawped at her car. Were they out of breath or shocked by its condition?

Lisa slowed down, almost to a standstill, lowered the passenger side window and waved. 'Nice day for it,' she shouted.

With feigned smiles, they looked ahead again and stuck their noses in the air but could not resist the urge to have another look.

'You two need to get out more,' she said. She wound up the window and then drove on.

A few seconds later, she had to slam on the brakes. It was either that or she would have crashed.

The lamppost was there, in all its concrete glory, in the middle of the path. By the time one of the joggers had taken her eyes off Lisa's car and turned her head to watch where she was going, it was too late; she had bounced off the lamppost and landed on her backside. The other jogger kept a straight face as she helped her friend get back on her feet.

Lisa saw the whole incident in her mirror. *I'm surprised the poor woman didn't knock herself out. She's going to have a sore head.* She stopped laughing, shook her head, checked her mirrors, and then drove on.

'What the ...' A caterpillar scurried along the dashboard towards her. Its legs moved in unison. She did not want the critter anywhere near her as anything with more than four legs tended to crawl wherever it wanted. 'How did you get in?' She sounded sincere as though she meant it no harm, but she had a sinister plan. Beside her, on the passenger seat, was an empty plastic bottle. Although the caterpillar did remind her of a character from a famous children's book, what she intended to do was anything but child friendly. As she drove on, she focused on the road and fumbled for the bottle. She found it and grabbed it. The caterpillar stopped as if it sensed what her next move would be, but before it had time to backtrack, she reached across and whacked it.

Part of the caterpillar was splattered on the dashboard. 'Nasty little creature.' She squirmed, glanced at what was left of it on the bottle and threw it into the passenger seat footwell.

The car jolted. She had hit what was probably the deepest pothole in the county. 'Someone, please, remind me why I pay road tax.'

Ahead, on the left-hand side, was a layby. She pulled in and got out.

Well, I can't put in a compensation claim against the caterpillar for whiplash, but I can against the council. She needed to ring Eliza to check everything was okay at home, which, she realised was what she should have done in the first place. She massaged her neck and shoulder, went to pull her mobile phone from her pocket, but it was not there. She patted her pocket to double-check before she looked in her other pockets. Nothing. The mobile phone was not on her seat either. She checked down the back, sides and underneath. Nothing.

As she straightened up, she hit the back of her head on the door frame. 'Damn!' She had not cursed because she had hurt her head. It was because she hated it when she did anything stupid. She rubbed her head, an automatic reaction, before she thumped the car roof with the side of her fist. She stepped back, put her hands on her hips and tried to gather her thoughts. *My mobile phone must have fallen out of my pocket on that driveway or in front of that window. I haven't got time to get it either. I'll have to go back later before those people get home from work. I can't leave any evidence laying around.*

She got back in the car and turned the key in the ignition. Several cars were on the road, but it was still quieter than usual. Aware it was only a matter of time until the dog walker reported her to the police, she pulled out.

It would take her a couple of minutes to get back if she did not have to make any more unexpected stops. Would the police catch up with her before she got back?

More people were out and about. Some paid particular interest in her car. *Why didn't I abandon the car and run back? I could've had everything sorted by now. Why do I keep making the wrong decisions today?*

A mobile phone rang. It sounded muffled and distant. She recognised the ringtone. It was the same as hers. It took her a moment to realise that was because it was her mobile phone. She remembered she had put it in her car boot, so she would not get disturbed at the funeral. She did not have time to stop. Perhaps whoever it was would leave her a voicemail. She would check when she got back.

A bang, like a small explosion, was followed by an incessant hiss. The driver's side front end collapsed. She steered to the roadside and came to a stop in a ditch. The airbags went off.

'Why didn't you go off earlier when I crashed into those cars? It would've saved me a lot of time in the long run.' She punched her airbag, grabbed the door handle, and opened the door into the path of an overtaking car.

The speeding driver swerved and sounded his horn. The noise lasted several seconds longer than was necessary.

She slammed the door shut. 'Sorry,' she shouted. 'And thanks for stopping to help.' She saw his silhouette through his rear window and watched as he gave her the middle finger. 'Charming. Let's hope *you* don't have an accident.'

She grappled with the airbags as she retrieved her handbag from the front passenger seat. She checked for overtaking vehicles, opened the door again, got out and slammed the door shut before she made her way towards the boot.

Her mobile phone was tucked inside one of her walking boots. She got it out and slammed the boot lid shut. *I'll ring the breakdown company later.* She locked the car and started to jog along the road.

*

The dog walker had got back to his SUV to discover someone had smashed into its rear. At first, he assumed the convertible driver was to blame, but considered it unlikely as the other driver was not there and their car alarm sounded out too. He noticed a lady driver, in a damaged car, pull out of a driveway. It did not take him long to work out what had happened.

He watched the lady as she drove away, and he followed on foot.

He took a photograph, on his mobile phone, of her damaged car and registration plate.

He waited for someone at the local police station to pick up the telephone, but no one answered. Maybe they were busy, or no one was there. He thought for a moment about what he might do next and decided to dial nine-nine-nine; the crazy lady should not be on the road.

With wide-eyes and pinned back ears, the dog felt its master's quickened heartbeat.

Oblivious to the car approaching from behind, the dog walker stood in the middle of the road.

The driver of the car had just finished a nightshift. He had driven the same car and worked the same shift for years, had never taken a day off sick, was used to the unsociable hours and yet he felt exhausted. He yawned, closed his eyes for a second, and fell asleep. His foot lowered on the accelerator, and he drifted to the right.

The dog heard the approaching car. It turned to look, yelped, and then scratched at its master's arm as it tried, in vain, to escape.

The dog walker took the mobile phone from his ear. He knew the difference between national and international tones, but that sounded strange, like he had tried to call a different world. He disconnected the unanswered call, looked down at his dog to see what was wrong, believed he held it too tightly and loosened his grip.

The dog took flight as if it had grown wings. It landed with a simultaneous yap, scrambled to its feet, and scarpered to safety as fast as its legs allowed. Its lead trailed behind.

The dog walker watched as his dog fled. He was about to follow when he heard the car. He turned round to look. With not enough time to get out of the way, the driver was less than a car length away. Time appeared to slow down. The dog walker's eyes widened, his mouth opened, and his body became rigid as he waited for impact.

The driver gripped the steering wheel. His seat belt kept him upright and pinned him against his seat. Sound asleep, with his head flopped forward, he ploughed into the dog walker.

The dog walker toppled backwards like the last skittle in a bowling lane. His mobile phone flew from his hand and landed in a roadside puddle. He landed with a thud on his backside. His head shattered against the road. His teeth clashed together. A sharp pain surged up his spine and down the backs of his legs. The circling stars above disappeared and were replaced with darkness.

Trapped underneath the car, he was dragged along the road. His shredded clothes exposed his shredded flesh.

When he opened his eyes, he discovered he was hovering over his body. He watched as his life drained away, yet he still felt the warmth of blood gush from the back of his head and the weight of the car on top of him.

The driver opened his eyes. He was shocked to discover he had dozed off. In all the years he had driven it had never happened before. He slowed down and wound down his window to try to keep himself awake.

Aware he had hit something, as the front end of his car bobbed up and down and plumes of steam rose from his dented bonnet, he pulled up at the roadside and looked down at his hands. They felt strange, somehow, like they did not belong to him.

The dog walker laid still. The dog, who had returned, licked its master's face to try to revive him.

Crows and magpies squabbled as they pecked at the trail left along the road.

In a catatonic state, the driver stared down at his hands.

It felt like an age before the black shadow withdrew from his body and ascended through the car's roof.

The driver's eyes widened. His body shook. He started to perspire. His stomach moved up towards his throat. He moved only his eyes to check his mirrors before he stared out of the windscreen.

The black shadow hovered, in front of the car, as though it wanted to be seen before it vanished.

The driver knew he had killed someone or something but did not get out of his car to check.

*

When the police arrived, they found him gripping the steering wheel as he stared out of his windscreen. Who would believe him when he tried to explain what had happened; when he talked of a black shadow that controlled him?

The driver was later charged with death by dangerous driving and sentenced to fourteen years in prison. Although in that instance, he was an innocent participant, he had previously got away with much more insidious crimes.

Chapter Three

Graveside

The vicar overlooked the incessant noises from the cars' alarms and the police car's siren as he uttered words of bereavement.

Elizabeth had wanted just one peaceful day, without any drama, to allow her to lay her daughter to rest. Of course, she had known the day would be anything but quiet.

As she stared down into what would be her daughter's final resting place, she realised she had missed the final prayer as those around her murmured, 'Amen.' The word flew around her head as if it refused to get carried along with the breeze.

She needed a drink; anything to dull her pain. But she already knew, from experience, that once the drink wore off, the ache in the pit of her stomach would return.

Susan's estranged husband, Karl, looked down at the brass plaque on the coffin's lid. He and Elizabeth had decided to have her birth name engraved on the plaque as the couple were going through divorce proceedings because she had committed adultery. He read her name repeatedly, in his mind, as though unable to understand his reality before he inadvertently said it aloud; however, no one turned to look at him.

He grabbed a handful of soil from the mound, beside the grave, and threw it on to the coffin lid; it echoed like the beat of tapping fingertips. 'Goodbye,

Susan.' He did not cry; not there, anyway, where the others would see. *I wonder if she can hear us. If she's counting how many times the soil hits the lid or if she's nearby watching us grieve. Does she know who's here? Does she know how numb I feel?* He stepped back and examined his hand; damp soil stuck to his palm and under his fingernails. He tried to wipe it off down his trouser leg.

Before the other mourners had chance to say their final goodbyes, Elizabeth asked them all to leave, except Robert. Polite, but hurried in her manner, she pushed them along as though they were intruders. She believed her pain was greater than anyone else's. Susan had been *her* baby. How could anyone know how she felt? How her heart ached like never before? She felt sure it would burst.

With his head lowered, Karl shuffled along the footpath. He turned and looked around the graveyard before he left. What had he expected to see? Had he wanted Susan to appear? How could he have known that was not possible as her soul was trapped, along with her lover's – William Oates (Bill), inside the black shadow. His last memory would be the two of them arguing; harsh words, spoken in haste, which could never be taken back.

Grandma Buckley looked concerned for her daughter, Elizabeth, but she kept quiet as she turned to link arms with her husband. Grandad Buckley looked ill and more frail than usual, like he might fall over if there was a sudden breeze. Unaware of what went on around him, he blew his nose into a tissue.

The couple respected Elizabeth's request and left. They would get a taxi to the airport, try to get an earlier flight back to Spain and then call her once they had landed to make sure everything was all right.

No one had mentioned a funeral wake. No memories would be shared over drinks and food.

The vicar had seen much grief in his time and knew when to console and when to stand on the sideline. With small pensive steps, he made his way back towards the chapel.

The vibes that emanated from Lisa, during the service, had made him nervous. He was relieved when she left early. Even though she had not said or done anything specific, he had felt scrutinised. He remembered a similar experience, but not that intense or inside his chapel. During the service, the chapel walls had appeared to draw closer and made him feel claustrophobic. He had remained composed throughout despite his lethargy and nausea.

He stopped beside the crypt entrance: a short warped wooden door with scuff marks and peeled varnish. Once access to the Sunday school where piled books and wooden toys gathered dust in one corner because no one took their little ones any more. He turned round, looked across at the Caplins and waited in case he could help them further.

The fine rain stopped momentarily.

Elizabeth, a broken woman, no longer held back her emotions. She fell to her knees on the mound of soil beside the grave, covered her face with her hands, and sobbed.

Robert, who was stood beside her, put his hand on her shoulder. He looked helplessly at her and then down at the coffin. In the past he had always avoided emotional situations and was not sure what he should do to comfort her. The last funeral he had attended was Diane's, his late wife, but he did not cry.

Elizabeth opened her fingers and peeked down at the coffin. 'Why did it have to be my Susan?' She moved her hands from her face and sniffled. Her eyes smarted. Her blotchy face was covered with tears and snot. 'Why was she the one to go first?'

He did not answer. He did not know what to say. He gently squeezed her shoulder and looked across at the vicar.

The vicar and Robert heard a distant thud. They turned their heads towards where the noise came from. Elizabeth appeared not to have noticed.

Chapter Four

Where's Peter?

Elizabeth's house was ahead, on the right-hand side, at the end of Caplin Lane. As Lisa went around the final turn, she saw the gate. Past the gate was a dead end with a high stone wall, partly covered with moss and climbing plants. Harry, the gardener, tended to the wall occasionally, but the moss and plants always grew back quickly. On the other side of the wall was the jetty.

Bushes and trees grew lakeside; some partly submerged while others grew on dry land. When it rained heavily and for lengthy periods of time, the lake spilled over and covered the lane, which made it inaccessible.

Her right calf muscle had cramped. She hobbled part way along the lane. *Oh, the joys of having to live in a human body.* She stopped for a moment and massaged her leg. *I really must start that diet and stop jumping in my car for those short journeys.*

The muscle cramp had eased by the time she reached the gate. She rested her back against the gate, leant forward and put her hands on her knees. She raised her head, grimaced, and waited a moment until she had caught her breath.

She had made the decision not to use the intercom as she did not want Eliza to know of her return. She heard Harry in the garden as he mowed the lawn. She pictured him as he pushed the lawnmower, backwards and forwards, in perfect straight lines, as he made sure each blade of grass was cut to a precise length.

She straightened up, stepped forward, turned round, and put her hands on her hips.

The gate was a solid metal structure with no protruding parts or holes for her to use as leverage, and there was no way she could climb over it without ladders.

She felt light-headed. Her chest had tightened. Her throat was sore. Her body was sweaty, and her face felt like it might burst into flames right before her head exploded. However, she did not let her aches and pains deter her. Hopeful she might find something to help her scale the gate, she looked around. There was nothing. *Come on. What would be the point in having a gate like this if it were going to be that easy to get over? Pointless wouldn't you say?*

As she contemplated how it might be quicker to wade into the lake and swim up to the jetty, the lawnmower stopped.

She hoped Eliza was inside the house as she called out, 'Harry.' She needed to grab his attention as she would have preferred not to tackle Eliza while dressed in wet clothes after a swim. 'It's me … Lisa. Can you open the gate?' She listened for his footsteps. *Did he hear me?* As she put her ear against the gate, she realised she would not be able to hear anything through the metal, and as she was about to call out again, his lawnmower started. *And there's your answer.*

A rock, about the size of a potato, was beside her foot. She picked it up and brushed away the loose dirt. A worm and several woodlice, which had been hidden underneath, scurried along the ground in search of another shelter. She struck the rock against the gate. It barely made a sound.

She stepped back and launched the rock over the gate. Why? She was unsure, but she had wanted to scream and pound the sides of her fists against the gate before she had thrown the rock.

She thought again how she might gain entry. The intercom was not an option, and she did not have any climbing equipment to scale the wall. There was only one other choice. *Well, this is where I'm about to be proven right. I'll show Mum and Robert how pointless this gate is when I swim up to the jetty, climb up, run through the garden, and walk inside their house.*

She turned round to face the lake. She planned to hide her mobile phone and handbag in one of the bushes. When she got to the other side of the gate, she would open it and retrieve them. But before she had chance to stash them, the gate started to open. She checked down the lane. No one was there. The gate stopped when the gap was wide enough for her to fit through. Had Eliza or Peter opened it? Or had it opened on its own? She never gave it a second thought as she squeezed through the gap sideways. She imagined what it might feel like if the gate closed and crushed her. Would she hear her bones break or feel her internal organs explode before she took her last breath? However, the gate did not close or squash her. It was only when she was safely through the gap that it closed again.

From the bottom of the drive, she watched Harry as he mowed the already pristine lawn. He had not noticed her. Had he not seen or heard the gate as it opened and closed?

She looked up at the house. No one was at any of the windows or either of the doors. Normally she walked up the drive, entered the house through the side door and exited through the French doors into the garden, but the incident appeared to have happened in the kitchen. She suspected Peter was in danger and needed to see for herself. She needed to catch Eliza in the act; however, whatever had happened was probably over, but maybe she would catch Eliza as she tried to cover-up whatever she had done.

A rose thorn snagged her sock and cut her ankle as she dashed through the flowerbed. She appeared not to notice. She made her way towards the weeping willow, hid behind it, lakeside, and peeked up at the house again. She needed to check Eliza had not seen her. It did not look like anyone was home or look like anything untoward had happened. What had she expected to see? A broken or blood smeared window?

At the far end of the lawn, furthest from the drive, Harry turned off the lawnmower, pulled a pair of scissors from his back pocket and crouched. He snipped a stubborn blade of grass that had evaded the lawnmower.

Hesitant to shout him again, she would wait until he turned round and then get his attention. But had he heard her thoughts as a second later he looked at her? She gestured for him to join her by the willow. He did; however, he looked apprehensive.

'Hi, Harry.' She looked up at the house. 'Is everything okay?' She had started to think Eliza might have taken Peter out somewhere and imagined the worst. *Maybe she's had to take him to hospital. What's she done to him?* But despite her inner anger, she appeared calm.

He nodded and then turned his head to check on what she was looking at.

'Have you seen Peter or Eliza recently?'

'No. Why? Is something wrong?' He rubbed the sides of his lower back.

'I'm not sure.' She shrugged. 'Have you heard anything? Any crying or any shouting?'

'No. Not that I've noticed. I've been in the garden since I got here. Not even been in the house for a drink or a toilet break yet.' He stroked the top of his head, which he always did when he felt nervous.

For a moment, she deliberated if he might know something, but decided it was unlikely as he had always been honest with her. He was as clueless as her. 'Listen, Harry, why don't you take the rest of the day off.' She smiled and looked around the garden. *What does he find to do all day anyway?* 'I've got a feeling something's not right and I don't want you to get dragged into whatever's going on.'

He frowned. 'Not, right?'

'I'm sure it's nothing; probably just me being paranoid, but all the same I'd prefer it if you weren't here.' She put her hand on his shoulder and looked him in the eye. 'There's nothing for you to be concerned about.'

'But what about Mr Caplin? What will he say when he gets home and finds I've left for the day?' He felt awkward. Any holiday was always agreed with Mr Caplin, and more than a day's notice had to be given.

'Don't worry about Robert. I'll clear your leave with him.' She nodded.

He knew something was wrong but did not pursue it. He always tried to avoid any type of confrontation. 'Is there anything you need help with before I go?'

'No, thank you, Harry.' She felt confident that whatever had happened, he was not an accomplice and was someone who preferred an uncomplicated lifestyle. She took her hand from his shoulder, inhaled audibly and as she looked up towards the house, her pupils dilated.

Although he had thought her words odd, he nodded and then made his way back towards his lawnmower. There was an order in which he tidied away his garden tools and he never deviated. He emptied the grass cuttings into a compost bag, which he had left at the top of the garden, and then pushed the lawnmower between two of the rose bushes towards the shed. The lawnmower shuddered across the drive. He collected the rake and shears from the lawn and glanced at her as he made his way back towards the shed. Neither spoke nor acknowledged the other.

Rattling sounds came from inside the shed as he tinkered.

Come on, Harry. Hurry up. What's he doing in there? Time to get yourself off home and put your feet up, old boy. She tapped her fingers on the willow's trunk.

A couple of minutes later, he appeared from the shed, put on his jacket, and turned round to lock the padlock.

She watched as he made his way towards the jetty with slow yet determined steps. He did not turn round, but he did wave half-heartedly. When he reached the jetty, he looked across the lake, pulled his mobile phone from his trouser pocket and made a call.

She was surprised to see he owned a mobile phone. *Don't most of the older generation prefer to use a landline or write? I wonder who he's calling. I don't think it'll be Robert. He wouldn't want to disturb him. It'll probably be a friend, who'll pick him up on their boat.*

The garden felt eerie as she peeked up at the house to make one final inspection. When she was sure no one looked out, she made her way towards the French doors. Had her dream been just that and not a warning sign? Were Eliza and Peter in the kitchen baking another batch of cookies? Or had something serious happened and she had wasted too much time on her journey back? She imagined his lifeless body on the floor while Eliza watched over him. *I'll never forgive myself if anything's happened to him, and I'll make sure she pays for it if it's the last thing I do.*

Stood outside the French doors, she glanced around the kitchen and into the living room. Neither Eliza nor Peter appeared to be there. Careful not to make a sound, she reached and pulled the handle down. The door was unlocked. She waited a moment to see if anyone would call out and felt like an opportunist burglar as she stepped inside.

The kitchen was immaculate. Everything was in its place, except for a couple of toy cars underneath the table: a police car laid on its side against a chair leg and a fire engine looked like it had been dropped; its ladders and front wheels had broken off.

As she made her way through the kitchen, she felt drawn to look up into the corner of the ceiling.

Peter was there. He was safe. To the sides of him, two of the small black shadows defied gravity and held him in position.

She put her index finger on her pursed lips and winked at him.

Chapter Five

The Confrontation

She stopped underneath the arch, between the kitchen and the living room, and looked towards the stairs. The house felt bigger somehow, like if she called out Eliza's name it would echo back at her. She no longer had to worry about Peter as the two small black shadows would protect him for as long as was considered necessary. All she had to do was locate Eliza and find out what had happened.

As she made her way towards the stairs, she held up her hand: a signal for the other three small black shadows, that hovered beside the fireplace, to wait. She held on to the banister, stepped on to the bottom stair and leant forward to listen for any movement upstairs. The house was quiet. Too quiet. She waited a moment before she called out, 'Eliza? Her tone was gentle as she did not want Eliza to be aware, she was on to her.

There was no response, not even a murmur. Perhaps Eliza had not heard, had chosen to ignore her or had been unable to move. The latter was unlikely because if anything had happened to Eliza, the small black shadows would have had no reason to protect Peter.

The stillness continued. *Has Eliza gone out and left him alone? Wouldn't Harry have noticed?* She was about to turn and walk away when she heard an upstairs toilet flush. She waited a moment to allow Eliza time to wash her hands.

The bathroom door handle clicked and then the door opened.

Her tone was serious as she called out again, 'Eliza.'

Eliza's footsteps stopped halfway along the landing before she continued to the top of the stairs. She saw Lisa at the bottom and feigned a smile. 'I'm coming.' She inhaled deeply and went down the stairs. 'You're back early.'

'Is everything okay?' Lisa looked around the room. 'Did Peter behave himself?' She pretended not to know of his whereabouts.

Eliza had hoped he might have appeared, from wherever he had been hidden, once he heard his mother's voice. 'Yes, everything's fine.' When she checked the sofa, she felt relieved to see it was still upright. 'And yes, he always behaves for me. He's such a good little boy,' she said as though she and him were the best of friends.

'That's good to hear.' Lisa hoped Eliza had noticed her feigned smile. 'We wouldn't want any harm to come to him, would we?' She considered how to continue without her words sounding like an accusation. 'Thank you for looking after him. I had this horrible feeling I needed to get back early because something awful had happened to him. I'm obviously mistaken.' She looked around the room again to allow Eliza a moment longer to confess any wrongdoing.

But Eliza did not respond.

'Where is he? Is he playing outside?' Lisa furrowed her brow. 'I didn't see him. Did I walk past him?'

Eliza gulped and looked down at her feet. 'I'm not sure,' she murmured.

Lisa narrowed her eyes. She had wanted Eliza to feel awkward as she felt sure she would confess under pressure.

'I mean … I know he's about. I'm just not sure whereabouts … exactly.' Eliza shrugged.

Lisa waited for her to elaborate.

Eliza raised her head and looked at her through teary eyes. 'We were playing hide and seek, you see.'

'Hide and seek?' Lisa paused. 'He loves that game; especially when he's playing it here at Grandma's house. There are plenty of places where he can hide.' She hoped she had led Eliza into a false sense of security. 'How long have you been playing?'

Eliza's eyes widened. 'Not long.' Her face reddened. Was Lisa aware of her lies? 'He's picked a good hiding place this time though.'

Unsure of how much longer she could keep up with the pretence, Lisa turned her head to the side and looked at the floor. 'How long were you in the bathroom?' She turned to look at Eliza again.

Vibes, like an invisible mist, lingered between them.

'Not long. I desperately needed to go to the toilet.'

Lisa liked that Eliza felt awkward. 'Have you checked the whole house?' She wanted to goad her further, scream at her, see how she enjoyed being bullied; however, it would not have the same effect as they were the same size; unlike Eliza and Peter.

'Yes, everywhere I can think of. Twice.'

'Have you checked the garden, all the outhouses and … the lake?' Lisa's eyes widened. She put her hand over her mouth and exaggerated feigned horror.

Eliza's bottom lip quivered. She had never thought to go outside. *Has he been outside the whole time?* She looked across at the French doors. One was ajar and it let in a cold breeze. Not able to remember if she had left the doors unlocked, she had not dared ask Lisa if she had used her key to get in.

She gave no sign when the voices returned: 'Peter will have tumbled into the lake from the jetty; he will have leant too far forward while gazing at his reflection.'

'Can the boy swim?'

'I bet he is dead and floats well. He will be face down, bobbing up and down, on the surface of the water, like a buoy at sea.'

'You might not have been the one to push him, you stupid girl, but you might as well have done. You have killed him. Now what are you going to do?'

'You had better hope the boy is still alive or I am sure you will meet with the same fate.'

The voices stopped. At that moment, she realised it was one voice that impersonated several.

'Well? Did you check? Have you looked outside?' Lisa said.

'No, I didn't.' *Why didn't I?* Eliza wanted to kick herself.

'We'll start our search upstairs.' Lisa looked across at the fireplace. The three small black shadows had gone. She assumed they had vanished, as a precautionary measure, in case Eliza had been able to see them. She made her way up the stairs. 'Where are you, Peter?' she called out.

Eliza followed but wondered why Lisa had not started her search outside.

Chapter Six

The Last Goodbye

With his hand still on Elizabeth's shoulder, Robert checked the time on his gold watch. His eyes widened. He leant forward and whispered in her ear, 'Do you think we should make a move?'

The vicar had gone back inside the chapel. He tidied the hymn books, straightened the kneelers on the pews and got ready for the next service; a more joyful occasion where an older couple were to be married for companionship. He had, however, left the chapel door wide open; an invitation should they need his help further, and to allow any residual negative energy to disperse.

Elizabeth moved her hands from her eyes. She struggled to keep them open as she turned her head to look up at Robert. She had started her day with a couple of glasses of red wine, which was not unusual, but she had also skipped breakfast because she was not hungry. Her lost appetite had lasted for days. The thought of food made her nauseous. 'I can't leave my baby girl here by herself. She'll be all alone and might get scared.'

He moved his hand from her shoulder and crouched beside her. 'We can stay a little longer if you need to, but I must get off to that meeting soon. I can't afford to be much later.' As he stroked her cheek, he saw her bloodshot eyes, flustered complexion, and runny nose.

With her hands on the mound, she tried to push herself up, but her arms started to sink. Before she knew what had happened, she was face down in the soil. She lifted her head straightaway. Soil was in her mouth and eyes. She spat several times and blinked quickly.

The mound started to slide outwards.

He straightened up, stood behind her and put his arms around her waist to stop her from diving headfirst into Susan's grave. As he held her, he imagined her laid on the coffin desperate to join her daughter. His feet started to slide sideways. He realised he had to act quickly, or they would both fall on to the coffin. He lifted her, guided her away from the graveside and made sure she could stand unaided. When he looked at her face, he realised she could not see him clearly as she squinted. 'I'd better ring for a taxi. I don't think you're in any fit state to walk home, do you?' he said.

With her hands, she tried to wipe away the dirt from her face and clothes. 'I think I need to get home and have a drink.' She straightened up as if she looked respectable again; oblivious that she had made herself look grubbier.

'That's the last thing you need.' He raised his eyebrows. 'What you need is a strong coffee and to get a decent meal inside you.' Aware she never ate enough, drank too much, and her problem had started before Susan died, he walked away, got his mobile phone from his jacket pocket and rang for a taxi. He glanced back at her as he spoke.

The conversation was loud and clear, but she chose not to listen because she was annoyed with him. He had insinuated that she had a drink problem. She wanted to scream at him and tell him he was wrong. Instead, she kept her thoughts to herself: *I'm not an alcoholic. I could do without a drink if I wanted to. I only drink because I enjoy it. I can stop anytime. I only need a small amount to help get me through. Anyway, what does he know? He's never had to go through the pain of losing a child. He's never had to go through what I'm going through.*

He returned and stood beside her. 'I've rung for a taxi. They're sending a driver over straightaway. They pulled him off another job he was about to set off for. Should only be a couple of minutes.' He doubted she had listened to a word. 'How do you feel?' He thought she looked a sorry sight. There was more soil smudged on her face as though she had fallen again. He tucked her hair, which was stuck to one side of her face, behind her ear, and wondered if he might be one of the reasons as to why she had become alcohol dependent. He realised his business trip could not have come at a worse time, but he enjoyed the lifestyle he had created for himself and did not feel any guilt.

Despite her unhappy face, her dirty appearance and inebriated demeanour, she continued to stand tall and nodded in response.

'That's my girl.' He checked for a clean patch on her forehead and kissed her.

As she looked across at Susan's grave, she burst into tears again. She had tried hard not to. She felt like part of her was gone, but she did not want the void to heal as she was afraid, she might forget Susan's face.

He felt helpless. He usually had every part of his life under control. He did not know how to help her to grieve or with her alcohol dependency. Should he get someone to talk to her? Would she accept help? He put his arms around her waist, pulled her towards him and hugged her. As he expected, she behaved cold at first, but she soon thawed. She reciprocated, hugged him, and rested her cheek against his chest. Her sniffling made him want to recoil, but he ignored his distaste and brushed his fingers through her damp hair.

Through the metal railings, which surrounded the chapel, he saw their taxi arrive. 'Our ride's here,' he said.

The driver looked across at Mr Caplin, raised his hand and nodded once.

Her tears had stopped, but her sniffling continued. She pulled away from Robert and wiped her palm, in an upward motion, on the underside of her nose, before she feigned a smile.

He passed her a folded tissue from the breast pocket of his shirt.

She made her way back towards Susan's grave and whispered, 'I'll see you soon.' Mindful not to get too close, she blew a kiss and waved. An unspeakable idea came to mind: *Should I open the coffin and take my baby home?* She took a deep breath and exhaled audibly. *Don't be an idiot. What a crazy idea.* She turned round and made her way back towards Robert.

They strolled along the footpath, which ran alongside the bottom of the graves, towards the archway. He scanned the birth and death dates on some of the headstones. Mindful his own demise could happen at any time, he still walked with a swagger. With slouched shoulders, she stared at her feet; hopeful the ground would open and swallow her whole.

The driver watched as they approached the taxi. He knew of their grief, had experienced the pain himself before, and chose not to smile or greet them. He got out, kept his head lowered, opened the passenger door behind him and walked around behind the car to open the other back passenger door. He got back in the car and waited.

Robert helped her into the car and closed the door. He got in behind the driver.

The driver knew their names and their destination. With no reason to disturb them, he waited until he had heard their seatbelts click.

A police car, with two officers in the front, slowed down as it passed by. With narrowed eyes, the officer, on the passenger side, studied everyone inside the taxi.

The taxi driver looked over his shoulder, pulled out and kept a safe distance from the police car.

The police turned on to a side road.

The taxi driver and Robert looked up the side road as they passed. The noise from the cars' alarms continued. Elizabeth appeared not to have noticed any of what went on as she stared out of the windscreen with a face void of emotion.

The driver knew the traffic lights ahead were broken as he had driven through them several times already. With no pedestrians around, he continued through the red light. He glanced in his rear-view mirror and noted Mr Caplin's concerned facial expression for his wife.

Blue lights flashed ahead.

The driver slowed down.

Two police cars blocked the road. Beside one of the cars stood three officers: each with furrowed brows. They chatted and pointed at something, out of sight, further along the road. In the middle of the road another officer gestured for the taxi to turn round.

No worries: a short detour would add only a couple of minutes to their journey. As the driver turned the car round, he tried to look ahead at what had happened. Robert did the same. With both of their necks stretched up, their heads moved to the left and right. But neither of them could see anything as the police cars blocked their view.

*

A short plump paramedic joined the three officers. Her ambulance was parked further along the road. She confirmed to the officers that the man laid in the road was dead and they had not tried to resuscitate him. Everyone, except for the driver who had knocked over the man, seemed relieved as it was obvious the dog walker's injuries were horrific.

Two of the officers and the paramedic made their way towards the body.

An officer crouched beside the body and searched through what was left of the man's pockets. He tried to find some form of identification as they needed to contact his next of kin. There was no mobile phone. He pulled out a well-worn leather wallet and looked inside. There was no cash, but there was a driving license and a few plastic cards. There was a passport sized photograph of a woman and a couple of young children – presumably, his family – and a telephone number scribbled on a scrap of paper. The officer passed the items to his colleague who was stood beside him.

Unable to make sense of what had happened, the sobbing driver was seated on a nearby kerb with his head in his hands.

The officer sat down beside the driver and started to question him.

The driver appeared not to have heard.

*

The trail on the road surface did not look like a spillage as it was red, intermittent and lumpy in places.

As the taxi driver made his way back along the road, a suited man inspected it. The driver swerved on to the other side of the road to avoid him. Luckily, there were no approaching vehicles. The road had been closed with cones and road signs ahead.

Had there been a human fatality? The police never closed the road for a dead animal; carcasses usually got thrown to the roadside or they kept getting flattened until they became part of the road surface. Was the trail where someone had been dragged along the road?

Elizabeth looked across at Robert. 'What's happened?' she said.

'No idea, but I'm sure there's nothing for you to worry about.' He put his hand on hers.

A yapping dog pursued the taxi.

She moved her hand from Robert's and turned to watch the dog through the rear window.

The panting dog stopped in the middle of the road. It watched as the taxi drove around the corner, out of sight.

As Robert and Elizabeth got closer to home, he saw what he thought was Lisa's car abandoned ahead. He leant forward. 'Could you pull over for a minute, mate?' He pointed at where he wanted the driver to stop.

The driver looked in the rear-view mirror, nodded, pulled in behind the car and switched on his hazard lights.

'Wait here. I'll only be a minute,' Robert said to Elizabeth.

With a face void of emotion, she turned to look at him. Of course, she had seen the car, but it had never crossed her mind who the car might have belonged to.

He opened the door a little and checked behind for passing traffic before he swung the door open and got out.

She watched as he made his way towards the abandoned car. From where she was seated, she could not see the registration number plate. She considered how the car looked like Lisa's, but that car had been in an accident.

He checked the ground around the car, except for the side that was inaccessible due to overgrown bushes. *What's Lisa been up to?* There were no broken light fragments or any other parts to show the accident had happened there. *And why did she leave the funeral early?* He looked through the driver's window and noted the airbags had gone off, no one was inside, and the keys were not in the ignition. *I wonder if she had anything to do with those car alarms going off that those police officers were going to investigate.* He made one final inspection of the car and the surrounding ground before he made his way back towards the taxi. *Why are the roads quieter than usual? Where's all the livestock gone from the neighbouring fields?* He looked up at the sky and then checked the treetops. *And where are all the birds?*

Elizabeth waited beside the taxi. She had realised the car was Lisa's. She felt annoyed and worried. Had Lisa orchestrated the accident to get attention? Where was she? Was she injured?

'Lisa's not in the car. Looks like she's had to abandon it. I'm sure she'll be on her way home.' He helped her get back into the taxi.

'Yeah, perhaps.' She pulled her seatbelt across and looked ahead.

He slammed her car door shut.

She jumped.

He crossed over the road. With his back to her, he reached into his pocket and pulled out his mobile phone. One of his acquaintances answered straightaway. He told him he needed him to collect Lisa's car before the police found it, and he explained the best route to take.

He got back in the taxi. 'Thanks,' he said to the driver.

The driver nodded, waited for Mr Caplin to fasten his seatbelt, and then he pulled out.

The rest of the journey home was quiet.

Chapter Seven

Unexpected Visitors

All of Peter's usual hiding places had been explored inside the house. Lisa and Eliza had looked everywhere they could think of; even in the places where he would find it an uncomfortable squeeze.

'He must have found a new hiding place,' Eliza said nonchalantly. She had expected him to leap out and when he hadn't, she felt a little concerned. *What if something serious has happened to him?*

The voice, which imitated several, reappeared: 'I tell you, Peter floats, face down, on the lake. You should have taken better care of him, Eliza. You cannot take your eyes off a child for a second; especially *that* child.'

'He will be all right. He is a bright boy. It is you who is rubbish at this game.'

'You should ask yourself those all-important questions: why is his mother acting calm? Why has she not tried to rip your throat out yet? She knows something. She is playing you and wants to make you nervous.'

Lisa made her way towards the French doors. 'He must be here somewhere.' She reached for the handle. 'He can't have just vanished into thin air.' She turned her head and glanced up into a corner of the ceiling.

Peter and the two small black shadows weren't there.

The shadows had made the decision to move him. It was the right choice as it would have been too risky to keep him hidden in full view. Eliza might have seen him and that would have been a difficult scenario to explain. But where had they taken him?

What had made Lisa look up? Eliza waited until Lisa was out of the room before she checked. There was nothing there. *Can she see something that I can't? That voice was right: she does know something, but what? Why's she playing games with me?* She followed Lisa outside into the garden.

Lisa looked towards the jetty. Harry had left. *Good. He deserves some time off. He's such a sweet old man and I don't want any harm to come to him; especially if something untoward happens.* She walked across the lawn, trudged between two of the rose bushes and made her way towards the top of the drive.

Eliza followed closely behind.

Why's she being so irritating? Lisa tried to ignore her. *And useless?*

All the outhouses and Harry's shed were locked. Peter would not have been able to get inside any of them, but Lisa checked, nevertheless. She rattled every padlock, knocked on the doors and called out his name. It was no longer a game of pretence. She needed to know where he was.

Eliza mirrored her.

Lisa narrowed her eyes and looked sideways at her. She wanted to say something, but resisted as she thought it pointless. *She's trying to annoy me and make me angry.*

But her worries worsened as she looked around and underneath the parked cars. She knew he was taken care of, but something felt wrong in the pit of her stomach. *Where is he? Where have they taken him? Why aren't they giving me a sign to let me know he's all right?* 'Okay, you've won, Peter. You can come out now.' She listened for a response.

She made her way between the rose bushes, across the lawn and stopped by the willow. As she looked up at its branches, she called out his name. *Maybe he's curled up into a ball. People are harder to see when they do that.* She looked around and made her way towards the jetty. He was nowhere to be seen.

Either he had not heard her or had ignored her. But why would he? Was he cross with her because she had left him alone with Eliza or because she had seen him with the shadows and had not tried to get him down? Was he afraid? Maybe there was a simpler explanation. Did he think the game was just that and his mother had called out his name to try to trick him out of hiding? Or was there something more sinister afoot? Was he trapped and unable to move? But she knew that was unlikely as he was protected; so why did she feel like something bad had happened or was about to happen?

She stood on the jetty. Relief washed over her. His body was not in the water.

It was unusually quiet for the time of day. Not a soul in sight except Eliza who stood beside her like an obedient lapdog. Where were all the tourists? Was there a local event on? If there had been, it was doubtful everyone would be there at the same time.

'Well at least we know Peter hasn't drowned.' Eliza exhaled, put her hands on her hips, and turned to look at Lisa.

Unable to believe Eliza's nonchalance, Lisa felt enraged. 'So, the thought had crossed your mind that my son might have drowned then?'

'Well … yes … but I knew he hadn't,' Eliza's voice trembled.

'How do you know he hasn't?' Lisa's words dwindled as she had started to believe her own words. 'His body might have sunk to the bottom.' She wanted to shake some sense into Eliza. 'And why were you angry with my son? What did my little boy do that was so bad you felt you had the right to scare him half to death?'

Eliza's eyes widened. She stepped back and put her hands out in front of her to try to protect herself.

'He was playing with his cars. That's what little boys do. They make noise, sometimes a lot. Why did that irritate you so much?'

How does she know what he was doing and what I did? Are there cameras in the house? 'I didn't mean to.' Eliza gulped. 'He wouldn't stop with those vroom noises and the voice I keep hearing drives me mad.'

Taken aback by Eliza's revelation, Lisa paused for a moment before she said, 'What voice?'

Eliza shook her head. 'I'm sorry, but I've not felt like myself for a few days. I keep hearing a voice and

I don't know where it's coming from.' Believing Lisa might have understood, she lowered her arms.

But she was mistaken.

Without any further thought, Lisa put her hands around Eliza's neck and shook her. 'How irresponsible are you?' Spittle sprayed over Eliza's face. 'You've endangered my son's life.' She tightened her grip and pushed her thumbs against Eliza's windpipe.

Eliza's face changed from red to purple. Her eyes glistened and bulged; their colour mirrored her skin. Her temporal veins resembled swollen earthworms and looked like they might explode if they were touched.

The gate at the bottom of the drive started to open. Elizabeth and Robert had arrived home. She clambered out of the taxi. He paid the driver along with a generous tip and a suggestive look that the driver should keep quiet about the abandoned car.

The driver nodded and then reversed up the lane.

Lisa had heard the taxi pull up and the gate open.

Unable to cry out for help or find the strength to pull Lisa's hands away from her neck, Eliza tried, in vain, to breathe. Angels in long white flowing gowns, hovering over the lake, were the last thing she saw before she passed out.

Elizabeth and Robert sauntered through the gateway. They looked down at the ground as they made their way up the drive towards the side door of the house.

The gate closed.

A dead weight in her grip, Lisa visualised Eliza's head as it tore away from its body, the head and spinal cord dangling from her hands. Reality intervened when she heard two sets of footsteps and turned to check. Whatever would Elizabeth think of her if she caught her with her hands around Eliza's neck? She released Eliza and watched her drop to the jetty.

Eliza sounded heavier than her actual weight as she landed on the timbers with a thud.

Elizabeth and Robert turned their heads to check where the noise had come from. They dashed towards the lake. When they arrived at the jetty, they discovered Lisa looking down at Eliza.

'What have you done?' Elizabeth shouted. She put her hand over her mouth.

What could Lisa say? She had been caught red-handed. It was obvious from the redness around Eliza's neck what had happened. She had planned to kick the body into the lake and allow everyone to think Eliza had drowned. *I don't understand: why hasn't my Curator Angelus sorted her out already?* She started to walk away.

'I asked you a question, young lady?' Elizabeth reached out to grab her, but missed; however, her fingernails caught the back of Lisa's hand. 'Don't you dare walk away from me while I'm talking to you.'

Robert stepped back. He had decided not to intervene. Eliza was only an employee, while Lisa was his stepdaughter, and even though she lived under his roof, she was not his responsibility.

As Lisa walked away, she wiggled her fingers and examined the back of her hand. There were three scratches, approximately a centimetre apart and an inch in length; not bloodied gouges, but they were swollen, and they smarted. She knew Elizabeth had not hurt her deliberately, but she still could not figure out why Elizabeth continued to show such animosity towards her.

One of Eliza's eyelids sprang open and then the other. Wide-eyed, she had not dared to blink or breathe as she felt sure Lisa's hands were still wrapped around her neck. She reached up and tried to pull Lisa's hands away. It took her a moment to realise Lisa was no longer there and the sensation of compressing fingers around her neck was in her imagination. She gasped for air.

The cut on the side of her hand, from where she had punched the bedroom wall, throbbed and she was not sure if the pain that ran from the cut to her elbow was caused by an infection or if she had landed awkwardly. She tried to get to her feet, but she was still too weak.

Lisa had heard Eliza stir. She stopped and turned round to check.

Robert noticed Eliza's struggle and decided to intervene. He dashed across and helped her get to her feet. He put his arm around the back of her waist and held her up. 'Are you okay?' he said. Was his concern for her or did he envisage a compensation claim?

She had not heard his question because the voice had returned: 'Are you going to let that *bitch* get away with doing that to you?'

'Who does she think she is?'

'You should finish her.'

'Give her a piece of her own medicine.'

The finger-shaped marks had darkened around her neck. Her face was blotchy, and the whites of her eyes were bloodshot. She would lean against Mr Caplin until she had regained some of her strength.

Lisa wondered why Elizabeth and Robert had taken Eliza's side and had not given her time to explain. The idea had never crossed her mind that her own behaviour was wrong.

She started to daydream: *Robert let go of Eliza and walked away. Elizabeth followed. Lisa and Eliza were alone. As though Eliza could not see her, she looked through her and tried to take a step forward, but her legs crumpled. Lisa saw an opportunity and tackled her. In slow motion they flew several feet before they dived into the lake.* The coldness of the water felt real and almost took her breath away. *They resurfaced. She pushed Eliza back under. Bubbles surfaced as Eliza struggled.* What might it have felt like if Eliza drowned, and her soul passed through her own. The fantasy was cut short. She took a deep breath.

'Are you going to tell me what's going on, Lisa?' Elizabeth pursed her lips.

Lisa looked around. No one had moved. She tried to recall the last time she had seen Elizabeth behave that way. It was like she looked at a different person. Elizabeth had never been one for confrontation or one to stand her ground. Had Lisa not realised how much she had changed too? Annoyed at Elizabeth's lack of concern for Peter's whereabouts, she said, 'Aren't you going to ask me where your grandson is?' Her voice quivered. Her arms shook. Her legs felt weak.

Elizabeth turned her head to look for him, a half-hearted attempt.

'Aren't you the least bit interested?' Lisa's eyes widened. *Are you really my mother? What's happened to you?* 'Remember Peter? My son? Your grandson?'

Again, Elizabeth did not answer.

'No, I don't suppose you're interested anymore.' She started to count to ten in her head, but only got to three. 'I can guess what he thinks when he looks at you: you're an embarrassment and a drunk. You're only interested in where your next drink's coming from. I bet you're thinking about it right now; that or your precious drinking partner. Well *fuck* you and *fuck* Susan. I'm glad the *bitch* is dead.' Lisa wanted to cry, but she stopped herself and folded her arms.

Elizabeth did not blink as she slapped Lisa across the face.

Many thoughts ran through Lisa's mind in the instant it took for her head to loll to one side: *Why's Susan the favourite? Why doesn't my mother care about me? Did she ever love me?* She lifted her head, moved it left, right, backwards, and forwards as if she exercised stiff muscles. She looked at Elizabeth and tried to smile.

With her hand still poised mid-air, Elizabeth was ready to lash out again.

Whatever happened next, Lisa was adamant she would not retaliate. There was a cut on her cheek. It was from Elizabeth's engagement ring that had turned round to the underside of her finger.

Elizabeth put her hand down, perhaps a moment of regret?

When Lisa prodded her cut with her finger, to check for blood, it opened further. In a circular motion, she rubbed her fingertip and thumb together and then licked the blood from them.

Since Mr and Mrs Caplin had returned, Eliza had regained some of her confidence. 'Peter and I were playing hide and seek.' She paused. 'And then Lisa came back and tried to kill me. He's hiding and I can't find him; that's all I'm guilty of.'

Lisa shouted, 'All you're guilty of?' She knew he would be all right but was annoyed by everyone's blasé attitudes. 'You need to tell them the rest, Eliza. You need to tell them what you did. Go on. You've not fully explained what you did to him to me yet.' But she did not give Eliza chance to answer. 'I'll tell you what you did do. You scared my little boy half to death and that's why he's hiding. At least, for your sake, that'd better be the case.' She stopped to take a breath and added, 'And if I'd wanted to kill you, trust me, you'd be a corpse already.'

'I think *you* need to go and take your medication.' Eliza sighed, raised her eyebrows, and rolled her eyes – all at the same time. 'And people say *I'm* the crazy one.'

'I'm not the one who can hear a voice.' *No, I make serious stuff happen to those who cross me.* Lisa realised how childish they sounded and thought back to the days when she squabbled with Susan. Memories flashed in front of her as if she was an outsider looking through a window.

'That's enough, Lisa,' Elizabeth said. 'There's never any excuse to mock someone; do you hear me?'

Transported back to the present-day, Lisa was unsure which time-period she found to be the most laborious. 'No, you're right,' she said, but her nod was exaggerated and went on for longer than was necessary. 'I'm sorry, Eliza.' She looked at Elizabeth again. Her words came out slow and loud as if she spoke to someone who was hard of hearing, 'Peter's missing and I'm the only one around here who seems to care. He's not playing any game of hide and *effing* seek. Something's frightened him and all I care about right now are his whereabouts and his safety.'

Robert moved his arm from Eliza's waist and waited a moment, in case she fell, and then he made his way towards the lawn.

Eliza touched her bruised neck and began to sob; a delayed reaction to her near-death experience or did she cry because she no longer had the security of him beside her?

Whatever the reason, Lisa thought Eliza's whimpering sounded pitiful. *Is she for real? Are they even real tears? Oh, she's good; I'll give her that.* 'Would someone *please* tell me where my son is?' But while she might have seemed calm on the surface, inside she wanted to scream.

'I don't know.' Eliza shrugged. She wiped away her tears with the back of her hand. 'I've no idea.'

Elizabeth fell for Eliza's performance and tried to comfort her. 'It's okay. Don't worry.' She put her arm around Eliza's shoulders. 'Everything will be all right, you'll see.'

Lisa watched as Elizabeth behaved like she had found Susan's replacement. *I know Eliza hasn't got a clue where he is; I don't even know. But why did she get angry with him? And why does my own mother act like she doesn't care about her grandson's whereabouts? What's going on around here? And why am I the one who's being made to feel like the outsider?*

Robert checked his watch again. Time had passed quickly; too quickly. He was late. *The situation between these three women appears to have calmed, and Peter will be okay. They're fretting about nothing. The lad has simply found himself a good hiding place.* 'Elizabeth,' he called out.

She turned her head and looked at him.

'Sorry, I'll have to get going.' He tried to look regretful.

She frowned. 'What?' She raised her eyebrows. 'Where're you going?' It was hard to work out if she was angry or troubled by his untimely announcement. She made her way towards him.

'My meeting with the guys in Glasgow.' He watched her approach. He did not have time for her to make a scene; he was already behind schedule.

'What meeting?' Her mind went blank. She had no recollection of a conversation about any meeting in Glasgow; especially one on the day of her daughter's funeral.

'Please don't start. I did tell you.' The last thing he needed was an argument. It was bad enough three women had had a heated dispute in his garden, and he'd had to get involved. In hindsight, he wished he had made his excuses and left as soon as they had arrived back at the house.

'Don't start what? When did you tell me?' She tried to recall and shook her head. 'I swear you've not mentioned the meeting to me before.' She wanted to get down on her knees and plead with him to stay, but she stopped herself.

'Will you listen to me? I've told you. I'm sure I reminded you a couple of days ago and I mentioned it to you before we left the chapel. You knew I'd have to leave straight after the funeral. This meeting's important. I can't get out of it and I'm already late. I've got to go.' But as he turned to walk away, he felt a rush of ice-cold air pass in front of his face and touch the end of his nose. The sensation took his breath away and stopped him in his tracks. Unsure of what he might find, he remained composed as he checked around, but there was nothing to see.

'No, Robert, I need you to stay here with me.' She tried to stall for time and appeal to his better nature. 'Maybe you thought you'd already mentioned it.' Her smile could not disguise the tears in her eyes.

He rolled his eyes and muttered, 'More like you were drunk and don't remember.' The instant the words had left his mouth, he regretted them and wished he could take them back. He turned to look at her and hoped she had not heard.

I'm not going to ask him to repeat himself. What'd be the point? If he didn't lie, he'd only say it louder and slower, and I don't want Lisa or Eliza to hear. I'd feel more of a fool than I do already. And why does everyone keep going on about me being an alcoholic? I know plenty of people who drink more than I do, and no one ever points a finger at them. She felt hurt, like he had betrayed her. She decided to stay quiet.

'I'll give you a call later; let you know if I'll be back tonight.' He kissed her cheek and wrapped his hands around hers. 'Okay?' He looked in her eyes and smiled.

A feigned smile followed her nod. She watched as he made his way through the French doors into the house. A minute later, he left via the side door with an overnight bag and made his way towards his car. A minute later, he had driven away. The gate closed behind him.

As she approached the jetty, she realised she should not have left Eliza alone with Lisa. But when she got there, Eliza was alone, and she looked weak and distant. 'Where's Lisa?' She looked around.

Unaware Lisa had gone, Eliza looked around too. 'I don't know.' She shrugged. 'I was watching you.'

The voice returned: 'Are you blind or stupid?'

'Impossible, Lisa cannot vanish.'

'You must have seen or heard something. Think.'

Elizabeth found it hard to believe Robert would have left for a meeting she was sure he could have cancelled or postponed. She needed a drink, more than ever, but wanted to prove her doubters wrong, so she resisted. 'Are you sure you didn't see which way Lisa went?'

Eliza shook her head.

'Will you be, okay?' Elizabeth pointed at Eliza's neck. She tilted her head slightly to one side and frowned as if she had inflicted the injury on Eliza herself.

Eliza nodded.

'Well, if, you're sure.' Elizabeth waited a moment before she made her way up to the house. She stopped short of the French doors when she thought she heard a car pull up on the other side of the gate. *Who could that be? I'm not expecting anyone. Maybe Robert's decided to come back after all. His conscience must have got the better of him and he's decided to cancel his meeting. Come on, you know him better than that; he'll have forgotten something.* The gate did not open.

She checked the intercom's monitor in the kitchen. She recognised neither the car nor the registration. She watched as the driver's door opened and a priest got out. The front passenger door opened, and a woman got out. She got closer to the monitor to try to get a better look at their faces. *I recognise her, but why would she be visiting me? I hardly know her and haven't seen her for years. Hang on ... now I think about it, did I see them outside the chapel earlier peeking through the railings?*

She pressed the intercom's speaker button. 'Hello. Can I help you?'

The priest's face drew closer to the camera. He started to mime.

'Hold the button in and then speak,' she said.

An intermittent crackle was interrupted by a high-pitched sound that lasted for several seconds. 'Ah … yes … hello, Mrs Caplin. We wanted to pass on our condolences.' There was an awkward silence before he spoke again, 'Mrs Caplin, are you still there?' He realised his finger was still on the speaker button and she would not be able to answer. He pulled his finger away.

'That's kind of you both. Thank you. But tell me, have you travelled all the way up from Beechwood just to pass on your condolences?' The noise from the intercom had left her with a constant buzzing in her ear that sounded like an angry wasp. She wiggled her little finger inside her ear.

'Oh no.' The priest sniggered. It sounded false like someone who had been caught off-guard. 'We were in the area anyway. Do you think we might come in? We would like to speak with you, face to face.'

The request seemed odd like he had told her only half a story. Why was he there? How did they know where she lived? Strangers did not usually call round to the house to see her, but one of the visitors was a priest and she did recognise the lady. What harm could it do to let them in?

The gate started to open. She walked down to greet them.

*

Despite her disagreement with Lisa, Eliza had waited for her to return. There had been neither sight nor sound from Lisa or Peter, so she made her way back up to the house.

Chapter Eight

Revelation

The priest held out his hand. 'Mrs Caplin, please allow me to introduce myself.' Brief eye contact was made. 'My name is Damian Ponder.' He turned his head and gestured. 'And this is my good friend: Melanie Willis.'

Elizabeth noticed that his musky aftershave did not mask his peculiar body odour. She found his gentle handshake hot, yet not clammy, and his skin felt smooth like silk. She shuddered; she had touched something similar before but could not remember what.

Melanie feigned a smile, looked at the ground and kicked a small pebble beside her shoe from left to right.

'Yes, I recognise Melanie from Beechwood, and please, I'd like you both to call me Elizabeth. I keep telling people Mrs Caplin sounds too stuffy.' She gestured for them to follow as she made her way up towards the side door of the house. 'What can I do for you?' She glanced at him. Her thoughts were elsewhere as they alternated between what Robert had said earlier and the altercation between Eliza and Lisa. *I wish this day would end and then I can hide and try to get some rest.*

'Like I mentioned before, we are here to pass on our deepest sympathies.' Damian's hand pushed the centre of Melanie's back as if she was his puppet. 'However, we would also like to discuss a matter of a

68

more delicate nature with you, if possible. I realise this is not an ideal time, but I do not think there will ever be such an occasion.'

Was Melanie there under duress? The situation made Elizabeth feel uneasy, but she was curious as to what he wanted to tell her. *What do they want?* As she opened the side door and stepped inside, she wished Robert was at home. They followed her through the house and into the kitchen. 'Can I get either of you a drink? A tea, a coffee or something a bit stronger?' She hoped one of them might be tempted to a tipple, so she could join them.

'Not for me, thank you.' He looked at Melanie who shook her head. 'Is Lisa at home?'

Elizabeth wanted to ask Melanie if she was all right, but something in the back of her mind told her not to. 'Oh ... so you know my daughter?' She looked out of the window. 'She's about somewhere, but I'm not sure where. Someone mentioned something about a game of hide and seek. I can't be sure. Maybe they aren't playing anymore.' She pressed her thumb and fingertips against her furrowed brow as though it helped her to think. 'I can't remember. I've just got back from the funeral and my husband has decided to go away on business at the last minute. My head's spinning with everything that's going on. I'm finding it difficult to keep track.'

'We are sorry to disturb you while you are grieving for your daughter, but it is vital we speak with you as soon as possible. We could meet somewhere later today. Just the three of us? Away from inquisitive ears.' He looked around the room, as though to check, and then back at her. He raised his eyebrows and waited for her to suggest a location.

'Yes, that'd be okay. But where?' Would he divulge unwelcome news? Did she want to hear it? Could she take any more? But she knew he would be insistent as he looked like a man who always got what he wanted.

'A park? Is there one nearby?' He knew there was as he had already checked the area.

Earlier that day, he had left Melanie alone, a few times, in various places. On one occasion, she was seated in a café, beside the window, and watched passers-by. On each occasion, he had returned with a smirk; delighted about something, but she did not ask what.

'There's a park around the corner. Go to the end of the lane and turn left.' Elizabeth gestured the directions. 'As you drive up, you'll see the entrance on the left. I'll meet you by the bandstand.'

'Thank you.' He nodded. Were his manners rehearsed, like an actor who read their lines on stage, or were they natural? 'We will see you there.' He did not wait for her to respond and led Melanie away, by her elbow, towards the side door.

Elizabeth followed. She wondered what the deal was with their relationship. Hadn't he said the two of them were close friends? It did not appear that way. What was the real story? Why did he have a hold over her?

Wide-eyed, Eliza was seated at the top of the stairs. Her mouth was open in disbelief. She had recognised his clear pronunciation, and it was not the first time she had heard his voice that day.

Elizabeth watched the supposed friends as they made their way down the drive. Neither of them looked back. The gate opened slightly and then closed behind them. It never crossed her mind that the gate had worked without her instruction as she went back inside the house.

Minutes later, Lisa re-emerged and joined Elizabeth in the kitchen. 'Mum, I'm sorry for what I said earlier about you and Susan. I was angry. You know I didn't mean any of it, right? I'm concerned I've done something else to upset you.' *Mum never gets herself this worked up. Is she really bothered about some little squabble I had with Eliza? No, there must be something else.* 'You seemed cross with me before the incident with Eliza. What's wrong, Mum? Can't we at least talk about it?'

Elizabeth jumped. She had not seen Lisa enter through the French doors. Neither had she heard any of what Lisa had said. Her mind was elsewhere: she contemplated what Damian and Melanie might want to talk to her about. He had mentioned Lisa. The meeting must have something to do with her. Had Lisa seen the recent visitors. She turned to look at her. 'Did you find Peter?'

'Yes, I know where he is.' *I wonder why Eliza said they were playing hide and seek though. She's trying to cover her own back, but why?* 'He's safe and well on Robert's boat, so there's no actual harm done.'

No actual harm done. Who is Lisa trying to fool? If we hadn't got home when we did, there'd have been a corpse to deal with. 'Good, I'm glad he's all right.' Elizabeth tried to smile, but there was too much on her mind for it to look genuine. Was he okay beside the water on his own? What if his fate mirrored Susan's? 'We don't want anything to happen to him, do we?'

It was difficult to ignore Lisa and Elizabeth's relationship had changed since Susan's death. Lisa had noticed. But had Elizabeth? And if she had, did she care? The days when the two of them gossiped over a coffee were in the past. Lisa wondered if they would ever be close again. 'Why didn't you want me to sit next to you at the funeral? There was plenty of room on the pew.' *I hope it's nothing to do with me. Maybe it's a marital problem or she's worried about her drinking. Maybe she feels like she's failed and doesn't feel like she can ask anyone for help.*

'*Please*, stop making everything about you.' Elizabeth frowned as she grabbed her reliever from the kitchen worktop. She held on to a chair back, inhaled on the reliever, waited a moment, and then inhaled again.

Convinced Elizabeth was not breathless and wanted to avoid giving her a straight answer, Lisa said, 'I'm not. You're acting like I've done something wrong. I know I lost my cool with Eliza earlier and I shouldn't have done. What if I apologised and promised not to do anything like that again?' She paused. 'But I know there's something else wrong; you were cross with me before that even happened. If

72

I've done something to annoy you, it'd be nice to know what it is, so I can put it right. Won't you at least let me try to make whatever it is right?'

Eliza strolled into the kitchen. She made it obvious she wanted to keep a safe distance from Lisa. But if she felt that nervous around Lisa, why had she waited alone on the jetty for her? One of Mrs Caplin's silk scarves was wrapped around her neck, and a couple of butterfly stitches held the wound together on her hand. She held her head as she rummaged through the drawers for aspirin.

'Are you going to ring the doctors to make an appointment?' Elizabeth said. 'It doesn't sound right that you keep hearing a voice.'

Lisa noted Elizabeth's caring smile.

Eliza smiled. 'Maybe,' she said. However, a doctor was not needed as the voice was not inside her head or a figment of her imagination. The voice, she had heard, was Damian's. How could she even try to explain what she did not understand herself? There was a packet of aspirin in the back of a drawer. She took out one of the blister packs, glanced sideways at Lisa and then left the room.

'I'm sorry, Eliza,' Lisa called out.

But Eliza, who still nursed her head, continued to make her way up the stairs.

'Mum, why won't you look at me?' Lisa moved closer to her.

Elizabeth's eyes were filled with hatred as she turned to look at her. She had not wanted to, afraid of what she might say or see something she had not noticed before. 'Because I don't want to,' she said with a spray of spittle.

'But why?' Lisa gulped to try to rid her throat of a prominent lump. The hurt was comparable to a dagger straight through her heart.

'Okay … you asked … so I'll tell you.' Elizabeth sighed. 'I wake up every morning and hope all of this is some crazy nightmare.' She gestured around her. 'Every time I close my eyes, I see Susan's body on the water.' She pointed towards the lake. 'A clear vision I'm forced to live through repeatedly, and the smell of her burnt corpse still fills my nose.' She sighed again. 'And I wish it was you who was dead and not *her*.' Her face appeared to relax, and her shoulders slumped.

Lisa watched as Elizabeth turned round and walked away. *Did she mean what she just said, or did I push her too far?* Lisa closed the French doors behind her and made her way towards Robert's boat – Diane. *I'm sure she didn't mean it. She's mourning and lashing out because she's upset and needs a drink. In a while, she'll feel awful and apologise. We're all feeling a little edgy. Yes, that'll be the reason.*

A little while later, Elizabeth looked out of the window. When she knew Lisa was nowhere in sight, she grabbed her jacket and left through the side door. She did not own a car and did not drive as she had not taken the time to learn. If she did not have to stop on the way and make small talk with anyone, it would not take her long to walk to the park.

Damian and Melanie were in the bandstand when Elizabeth sauntered through the park entrance. Because no time had been arranged, the two of them had headed straight there. They made their way across to greet her. Melanie seemed anxious. He seemed eager.

In silence, the three of them made their way along the path towards the pond where a family of ducks fed on some leftover scraps of bread. A red squirrel ran in front of them and scurried up a tree. Several pigeons scattered and took flight.

They strolled around the pond. Elizabeth was closest to the water. Damian was in the middle. Melanie was on the outside. He interrupted the uncomfortable silence, 'I expect you are wondering why we need to speak with you, Elizabeth.'

'Well, yes,' she said. 'I have to admit, the thought had crossed my mind.'

With a small gap for him to get by, a cyclist hurtled past them on the outside with a whoosh. Taken by surprise, Melanie gasped. Damian did not notice her alarm or the cyclist while Elizabeth knew Melanie must already have felt anxious about something.

'As you have no doubt already guessed, the matter concerns your daughter Lisa.' Damian seemed eager to get to the point. He had succeeded in his mission to get her away from Lisa and did not want to waste his opportunity.

'I had a feeling it might.' She glanced across at Melanie who was looking down at her shoes. *Why's she even here?*

'It is a lengthy tale we must tell you. I do hope you can spare us some of your time.' He tidied his hair to the sides with his fingertips.

'Yes, of course.' She found him hypnotic. She had noted his clear pronunciation but could not place his accent. He sounded too posh for Beechwood; only people who had moved into the area sounded like that.

Again, he got straight to the point. 'How much do you know about your daughter?'

She thought the question strange and frowned. 'I'm not sure I understand. In what respect?'

'I am sorry. Let me ask you the question in another way. Are you aware of who your daughter is *and* what she is capable of?' Aware it was unlikely she would know the answer, he raised his eyebrows.

'No, not one hundred percent, but I'm sure no parent knows everything about their child. Why would they want to?' She furrowed her brow further. Where were his questions leading? She thought him odd. He could have been anyone and his priest attire a facade. The only reason she had agreed to meet with them was because she had recognised Melanie.

'Would you believe me if I told you she is a powerful being?'

'Listen, I came here to meet with you because you had something important to tell me. If all you're going to do is waste my time, I might as well go home.'

'Would you at least listen to a few examples of what she has been involved with and, more often than not, instigated?'

This priest is unhinged. She noted he never blinked. *Why did I agree to meet up with them?* She started to walk away.

'She watched Mel's daughter, Vicky, as she was murdered, and she did nothing to help.' He raised his voice; he had to make her listen. 'She hid behind a bush and watched from beginning to end, every gory detail. What type of person would do such a thing?'

She stopped and thought for a moment before she turned to face him again. 'How was Lisa supposed to stop someone from getting murdered?' She felt a twinge of guilt as she glanced at Melanie; she had not meant to refer to Victoria as just a someone. 'But I still don't understand how that makes her a powerful being.' She looked at the ground for a moment. 'So, Lisa knows who the culprit is?' She frowned. 'But why has she never mentioned anything to me?'

'Oh … Lisa knows all too well who the guilty party is and, what's more, many others have died because of her.'

'Lisa?' She placed her hand on her chest, over her heart. 'My daughter? You're telling me she's an accessory?' She shook her head. 'Are you sure you've got the right person?'

He nodded and watched as she tried to take in the revelation.

She needed confirmation and looked at Melanie again.

It took Melanie a moment to raise her head and turn to look at her, but when she did, she nodded.

In silence, the three of them made their way towards a wooden bench. An artificial red rose had been placed beside a brass memorial plaque: a local lady who had loved to sit and feed the birds.

He sat down between Elizabeth and Melanie. Together, they watched the ducks.

Elizabeth turned her head to look at Damian. What if she knew the person in question? Her voice trembled as she said, 'Who murdered Vicky?' *Maybe it was him. That's why he's gone to all the trouble of tracking Lisa down. But the murder happened years ago. Why would he bring it all to the surface again if he's got away with it for so long? And why get me involved? What if he's trying to find out how much I know?* 'How do you know what Lisa saw if she's never mentioned any of it to anyone? How do you know she was there? And what are these other matters she's *allegedly* been involved with?' Did she want to catch him out or did she want to know the answers?

He started to explain every incident with precise dates, times and named individuals. He never appeared to pause for breath.

At first, she listened; although, most of what he had said sounded farfetched. Some of the victims had in fact taken their own lives. *He's talking nonsense. He's got his information from the newspapers.* Her thoughts drifted back to the drink until she heard Susan's name mentioned and then she started to listen again. He described every gory moment; some of the details she had not been privy to. Her stomach turned. *How does he know? Was he there?*

'In case the thought had crossed your mind, Lisa is not possessed; although, there are many people who do not realise that they are. Your daughter is, for want of a better word, a demon. Of course, she looks normal on the outside, but she would, would she not? The ones who appear more innocent are more likely to be evil; the perfect disguise.'

Is that right? 'How do you know all this?'

'I am a priest.' He looked down at his attire and gestured. 'It is my job to know.'

A gut feeling left her unable to pinpoint why she was unsure about him. Not the religious type she had, however, attended a Church of England School; therefore, it was second nature for her to respect anyone who was dressed like him. *But even if Lisa was involved in the murder of all those people, she wouldn't kill her own sister, would she?* 'Why are you telling me all this? I'm not sure what you expect me to do.'

'I give you my word, she *did* kill your daughter.' He paused. 'I realise I am a stranger to you, but I am also a man of the cloth. What conceivable reason would I have for lying to you?' His eyes narrowed as an idea popped into his head. 'I could walk with you around your town, if you like, and point out some individuals who are either possessed or are a demon, but you would find me even stranger than you do already.' He paused again. 'Maybe you need more time to come to

79

terms with what I have told you. But the choices are quite simple: you can decide to ignore what I have told you or do something about it. If you conclude I am telling you the truth, I could help you if you like; you only need to ask.'

Throughout their conversation Melanie had remained quiet. Any passer-by might have assumed she was not with them. However, she had listened to every word as she continued to watch the ducks go about their carefree lives.

Elizabeth leant forward, looked across at her and said, 'What's your opinion?'

An uncomfortable silence followed.

Elizabeth waited.

Melanie opened her mouth as though she was about to speak, but when she looked at Damian, she changed her mind.

'You must have an opinion; otherwise, why did you bother to come here?' Elizabeth felt like her head was spinning. Why didn't Melanie answer? Did she have nothing to say? She needed to know what Melanie thought. Who else could she turn to? Robert would laugh at such a story if he were around to tell.

Damian gave Melanie permission to speak with a nod.

Melanie took a deep breath. 'I believe everything Damian's told you.' She bit her bottom lip, as though she contemplated, before she continued, 'I must admit, I didn't at first. The whole thing sounded ridiculous, but when I'd had time to think, everything made sense; like a jigsaw with all the pieces slotted together. Give it time and I'm sure you'll think the same.'

Although Elizabeth did not like the answer, she had asked for Melanie's opinion. But there was still no evidence; only the word of an aged man who was dressed like a priest. There had to be more to it. What did Melanie stand to gain? She looked at him and said, 'What do you think I should do? It's not like I can go to the authorities; I'd be wasting my time. Can you imagine what they'd say? I'd be a laughing stock.'

Melanie tried to imagine what she would do if she had been put in the same situation with Victoria. 'Maybe you could ask Lisa outright?' She paused. 'If you confront her, she might confess everything to you; after all, you're her mother. If she knows you know, it might prevent her from doing anything again.'

'But if she's done what you say she has, and she is what you say she is, how do you know she won't kill *me*?' Elizabeth said to Damian.

He could not answer.

What was the time? She had not expected to be out for so long. After what had happened earlier, leaving Lisa and Eliza alone was not her best idea. 'Listen, thanks for drawing my attention to the situation, but I'd better be making tracks.'

'What will you do?' For the first time that day, he seemed desperate.

'I don't know.' She shrugged. 'Like Melanie said … I need more time to think.'

81

A wide-eyed Damian and a more relaxed Melanie remained seated. They watched Elizabeth walk away.

'Whatever you decide, *please*, be careful,' Melanie called out.

Elizabeth did not turn round, but she did wave.

A cold breeze blew across Melanie's face. She shivered and looked at the pond where the ducks had been. Had they waddled or flown away?

Elizabeth made her way towards the park entrance. When she reached the gate, she stopped and turned round to look at Damian and Melanie. From what she could see, he was still watching her. She was reminded of a film she had seen many years before. What was the title? After many years of marriage, the wife could take no more of her husband's controlling ways. She devised a plan and drugged him. While he was unconscious, she tied him up, hauled him into the cellar and locked the door. Every day, for weeks, she tortured him in unusual ways before she grew bored, so she finished him, or did she let him starve? How did that film end?

She tried to gather her thoughts as she made her way home. *I'd know if my daughter was a demon, wouldn't I? There'd be warning signs.* She shook her head to try to shake away the idea. *Wouldn't she look different to the rest of us? Wouldn't she have two little horns on the top of her head or redder, shinier skin. What about a pointy tail?* Her pace slowed. *But how did Damian know every detail of Susan's death?* She felt panicked and started to gasp for breath. *It can't have been Lisa who killed Susan. She was in Beechwood when it happened; I spoke with her on the hotel's reception phone. Hang on; did he say something about an accomplice? A Curator Angelus?* She leant against a wall and rested for a while.

Before she continued, she checked behind to ensure Damian and Melanie had not followed.

*

She pressed the gate's intercom button and waited for someone to let her in.

Her fears grew when no one answered or opened the gate. *What if something bad has happened while I've been out?*

Eliza's voice came through the speaker. The accompanying crackling sound made it hard to understand what she had said.

The gate opened slightly.

Elizabeth squeezed through the gap. The gate closed behind her. She waited at the bottom of the drive. *Where's Harry?* It looked like no one was home as she made her way up the drive. *I don't think I saw him when I got back from the funeral either.* She glanced across at the outhouses and the shed. They were all locked. 'Harry,' she called out.

The side door of the house opened. Eliza's head appeared around the doorframe.

'Eliza, where's Harry? I've shouted him, but he didn't answer.'

Eliza stepped outside on to the doorstep and shrugged. 'No idea.'

'And where's Lisa and Peter?' Elizabeth made her way into the house. She glanced around the living room, up the staircase and into the kitchen. 'It's quiet. Has something happened I need to know about?'

'Sorry, Mrs Caplin, I've not seen anyone for a while.' Eliza followed her into the kitchen.

Elizabeth turned round and put her hand on Eliza's forearm. 'You've got nothing to be sorry about. And how many times do I have to tell you, I'd like you to call me Elizabeth. Mrs Caplin sounds too formal. I've come to think of us as more than employer and employee; haven't you?' She smiled.

Eliza nodded.

But Elizabeth's smile disappeared when she turned to look out of the window at the lake; Damian's detailed description of Susan's murder came to life as if she witnessed the incident first-hand.

Eventually, the living nightmare ended. She held out her hands in front of her and tried to steady her shakes. Her heart raced and pounded against her ribs. Her pulsating headache made her nauseous.

Eliza could see Mrs Caplin was unwell and she wanted to help her.

Unsteady on her feet, Elizabeth made her way across the kitchen towards the wine cellar door. She opened it, flicked on the light switch, and used the handrail to guide her down the steep stone steps. The stale smell that usually greeted her was combined with another that she could not place; perhaps an animal had got in, hidden, and died. She tried to ignore the smell as she made her way towards one of the racks on the opposite wall. *One glass of wine won't kill me. It'll help me feel better. That can only be a good thing, right? It'd be better if I wean myself off the stuff rather than cold turkey. I've heard other people say that's the best way.*

She chose a bottle of Cabernet Sauvignon. A layer of dust had settled on one side. She tried to blow the dust off as she made her way back up the steps. *I'll ask Eliza to wipe all the bottles with a damp cloth. I'll see if she can find the source of that smell before it gets any worse. But I'll leave that for another day.*

Eliza watched her put the bottle on the worktop.

'Would you like to join me? I think we deserve a drink after the day we've had,' Elizabeth said.

'No, thank you, I don't like to drink while I'm at work.' Eliza grabbed a wine glass from the drainer and passed it to her.

'Please, Eliza, I'd like it if you joined me.' She glanced at the floor. 'I know what people are saying about me: I drink too much. But at this moment in time, I couldn't care less.' She raised the empty glass and continued, 'I need a friend.'

Eliza took another glass from the drainer and placed it beside the bottle. 'Okay, thank you, but make it a small one.' She demonstrated how much with her thumb and index finger. Red wine was not her favourite drink. When she went out with friends, she usually drank vodka, lime, and soda.

Elizabeth filled her glass close to the rim and half-filled Eliza's. 'What do you think of my daughter?' She took a mouthful of her drink, gulped, licked her lips, and then studied her glass. 'Be honest. I won't get angry. I know she's not your favourite person right now, but what do you think she's capable of?'

The mad cow tried to kill me. She scared the life out of me. That was what Eliza had wanted to say, but her chosen words came out different: 'I don't know Lisa well enough to comment. I'd have reacted in the same way if I thought someone had hurt my child. She reacted like any mother would put in that situation.' It was doubtful Mrs Caplin would have coped with the truth. She hoped she would not probe her further.

Elizabeth was not assured; her narrowed eyes were a tell-tale sign.

They sat down at the table.

Eliza, who was convinced she would never get used to the sharp taste of red wine, pulled a face every time she took a sip.

Elizabeth guzzled her wine like someone who drank from a water bottle after days lost in the desert. 'Will you be reporting what happened earlier, between you and Lisa, to the police?' She noticed Eliza had hardly touched her drink. She put her empty glass down and reached for the bottle. 'I wouldn't blame you or try to talk you out of it if you decided to. I know I would if it'd happened to me.' She poured herself another glass.

'I won't be going to the police. That's why I've decided not to go to the hospital to get checked over. Like I said before, I'd have reacted in the same way. Plus, I don't want there to be any animosity between any of us.' Eliza ran her fingertip around the glass's rim. 'I'm sure, in time, everything'll calm down and it'll be like nothing happened.'

'I wouldn't blame you if you changed your mind. Lisa can't behave that way and expect to get away with it.' Elizabeth thought about what Damian had told her. 'I've got an awful feeling she might have been getting away with too much for too long.'

'I think I'd prefer it if we forgot about the whole incident.' Eliza fumbled with the scarf to ensure her bruises were still covered.

'Okay, if that's what you want.' Elizabeth gulped another mouthful. 'But do you think there's something different about her?' She needed someone she knew to give her their honest opinion.

Eliza saw the frustration on Mrs Caplin's face and did not think it wise to give an honest opinion; it would make matters worse. 'I think there's something different about everyone if you look close enough. Wouldn't it be a boring world if we were all the same?'

'Do you think she could be a demon?' For a moment, Elizabeth believed someone else had asked the question.

Eliza's eyes widened. She had always been a sceptic of the supernatural. *Wow. Mrs Caplin needs to slow down with her drinking. Lisa might be a bitch, but asking if I think her daughter might be a demon is taking the craziness to a whole new level.* 'A demon? You mean like a monster from Hell?' She kept a straight face and then recalled Damian's voice.

Elizabeth nodded.

'I'm not sure there is such a thing. I don't know what I believe. I've always found the philosophy of the Biblical Heaven and Hell a bit hard to get my head around.'

Elizabeth finished her glass, poured herself another and topped up Eliza's glass with the dregs from the bottom of the bottle. She had not eaten all day, so the wine had the desired effect and had eased her withdrawal, although she had started to slur a little. 'I was told today that my daughter is a demon; admittedly, by someone I've only just met: a priest. But why would he need to lie?' She shrugged. '*Apparently,* she's responsible for many deaths going back years. I want someone to tell me what I'm supposed to think and what I need to do about it if anything. Should I act on what he told me or ignore him?'

Eliza felt the right thing to do would be to replace Mrs Caplin's drink with a strong black coffee, but it was not for her to do.

Neither of them had seen Lisa on the other side of the French doors with her face pressed against the glass.

Undecided if to enter as she was probably the topic of conversation, she opened the door, stepped inside and left it open behind her. A chilly breeze followed.

Elizabeth and Eliza turned their heads to look at her. Neither made eye contact. Eliza bit her lip.

The room's aura heightened.

Lisa made her way towards the refrigerator and grabbed a small carton of orange juice for herself and a small carton of milk for Peter.

Elizabeth's shoulders stiffened. 'Do you know where Harry is?'

'Yes, I told him he could have the rest of the day off.' Lisa closed the refrigerator door, turned round, and did not look at either of them as she made her way back towards the French doors. She stepped outside and closed the door with her foot.

Elizabeth and Eliza jumped up, ran across to the window and watched Lisa swagger towards the lake.

By the time Lisa had reached the jetty, Elizabeth's jaw had tensed, and her nostrils flared. 'Lisa *is* responsible for Susan's death; I know she is. And who gave her the authority to allow my staff time off?'

'But how's that even possible? Wasn't she in Beechwood when the accident happened?'

'She has an accomplice. Her *Curator Angelus* carries out the necessary task. She doesn't even need to get her hands dirty or be there. There have been occasions when she hasn't even found out until after the event.' Elizabeth narrowed her eyes. 'What's more, I'm pretty sure I've seen her guardian angel and more than once.'

'Was it that priest that told you all this?'

'Yes. His name's Damian Ponder. I'd never set eyes on him before today. He was with Melanie Willis. I recognised her from Beechwood. Her face was on all the newspapers years ago when her daughter, Vicky, was murdered. The police never did catch her killer. There weren't any photographs – too gruesome – and the report was barbaric; I chose not to read it. I remember parents up and down the valley were terrified the same thing would happen to their children. It was all everyone talked about for months. Parents tried to keep their teenagers indoors, but they'd sneak out, meet up, and go to the waterfall where the murder took place.' She thought she had been lucky to get her two daughters through that time unscathed, and she shook her head.

'Do you believe what this Damian's told you?' Eliza took another sip of wine; accustomed to the taste, she no longer pulled a face. 'I'm pretty sure Susan's death was accidental.'

'I know it sounds ridiculous, doesn't it? But I also know what I've seen.' Elizabeth paused. 'I know what you're thinking, but I'm pretty sure I've seen her guardian angel when I've been sober as well.'

'It does sound ridiculous, but don't forget, I'm the one who hears a voice, so I can't comment can I?'

'You must make an appointment to see your doctor.' An uncomfortable silence followed. Elizabeth continued, 'This is going to sound awful, but sometimes, I wish Lisa had never been born.' She paused. 'When I look back, I think I should've had her aborted. If she is a demon, I should have listened to everyone who pleaded with me to do the deed. At the time, I thought they were all being nasty, but maybe they knew something I didn't.'

The landline started to ring. They jumped.

Elizabeth made her way towards the living room and picked up the handset. She had expected to hear Robert on the other end of the line. 'Hello. Is that you, Robert?' She waited a moment. 'Who is this?' Someone was there; she heard heavy breathing. She put the handset down. 'Not sure who that was.' She shrugged and made her way back towards Eliza.

'Do you think the priest used the word *demon* when he meant to say *evil*?' Eliza had given more thought to what Mrs Caplin had asked her. 'Because I believe a lot of people have an evil streak, in fact most people. I'd say Lisa has a short fuse, but I find it hard to believe she was somehow involved with the death of her own sister.'

'He definitely used the word *demon* and not *evil*. The two do have similar meanings, but I'm sure a priest would know the difference.'

The landline rang again.

'I'll get it.' Eliza made her way towards the telephone. A gust of wind almost knocked her off her feet. Every internal door slammed shut in unison. Paperwork, which had been piled beside the telephone, was strewn on the floor. She brushed her hair from her eyes with her fingers, picked up the handset and said, 'Hello. Who is this?'

The line crackled at first until a voice came through. 'Eliza? Is that you? Can you hear me? Is Mrs Caplin not at home?'

'Yes, Mr Caplin. She's coming now.' Eliza gestured to Mrs Caplin and waited until she had taken the handset from her. She made her way back towards the kitchen and sipped her wine.

'Yes … one glass … I suppose … no, I've not seen him … okay … see you tomorrow.' Elizabeth sounded formal like she spoke with a work colleague. There was no *I love you* or a blown kiss at the end of their conversation. She put the handset down. Her hand hovered over the telephone. She tried not to cry and bit her bottom lip. A moment later, she straightened up, turned round, and went to join Eliza.

She picked up her glass, tipped what was left of her drink down the sink and then did the same with Eliza's. She stared out of the window at the lake. Images of Susan's death played on a loop.

Eliza watched her.

Chapter Nine

The Tip-Off

There was no siren. It was the blue flashing lights that caught Elizabeth's attention.

She wondered why the police officer, who had been parked outside the gate for some time, had not got out of his car and used the intercom. It was doubtful he was there for his tea-break. She decided to open the gate.

The officer drove through the gateway, stopped part-way up the drive and turned off the engine. He swung his door open, got out and slammed the door shut. He made sure he looked presentable, brushed his shoulders with his hands and then made his way towards the side door. He looked around warily. Had he expected someone to jump out?

From the doorstep, she watched him approach. He was tall and well-built. She guessed he was in his late twenties, still lived at home with his parents who had to re-stock the refrigerator and cupboards daily to keep him fed.

He introduced himself.

She invited him in.

Eliza had seen the flashing lights and made herself scarce. If questioned, she would deny any knowledge of Mr Caplin's stash of drugs or confirm any of the rumours. She looked at her blood on the carpet as she scrubbed and wondered how she would explain the hole in the wall.

I wonder if this officer's here about Lisa's car. Elizabeth decided not to mention the matter in case she was mistaken. 'Would you like a tea or a coffee, officer?' For someone who had just buried a daughter, discovered the other daughter was a demon, was married to someone who was always away on business and treated her like a random object he picked up and put down when the mood took him, she seemed calm.

He shook his head. 'No, thank you, Elizabeth.'

He knows my first name; not sure if I should feel flattered or be concerned? Aware he would smell the alcohol on her breath, she tried to keep her distance. 'How can I help?'

*

Lisa, who was still on *Diane*, had seen the police car and watched the officer as he made his way towards the house. *The police have found me quicker than I thought they would. Did I leave evidence in my car with this address on? A bit careless of me if I did. But in my defence, my mind was on a more important matter at the time.*

A wool blanket was draped over Peter's legs as he laid on a wooden bench on deck. With his back to her, he picked at a small patch of peeling paintwork. He had not said a word since she found him. She had apologised, promised never to leave him behind with Eliza again and tried to explain the black shadows would never hurt him or allow him to come to any harm; they were his friends, but he remained dubious.

The silence continued. Her attention alternated between him and the house. She considered what the

94

topic of conversation might be between her mother and the officer.

*

'I wanted to have a quick word with Robert, if he's at home,' the officer said. He looked around as though he expected Robert to appear when his name was mentioned. 'I noticed his car wasn't parked outside, but that doesn't mean he isn't here, does it? I tried to call him on his mobile phone, but he didn't answer.' He had started to babble. 'Maybe his car is in the garage or one of his acquaintances has borrowed it.' A chill blew through him, made him shiver and fall silent.

Surprised the officer had asked after Robert, Elizabeth said, 'He's not here. He's away on business.'

'Do you know when he'll be back?' His teeth started to chatter like a child's wind-up toy. 'Although, I have to add, there's nothing for you to concern yourself with.' He noticed she did not appear to have felt the cold while every hair on his body had risen in their collective search for warmth.

She wondered why he looked cold. 'I've spoken with him on the phone. I'm not even sure where he's gone.' *Why don't I know? Did he tell me? Why didn't he tell me? Why didn't I ask? There's no way this officer believes a word I'm saying.* 'He did say he was due to come back sometime tomorrow. He didn't give me a time though. Would you like me to ask him to contact you if he calls me again?'

He looked across at the French doors as he considered the quickest exit. 'No, that won't be necessary, thank you.' His skin had turned a pale shade of blue and his smile was more of a grimace.

She imagined icicles on the end of his nose and a thick layer of frost on his eyelashes. 'Is there something I can help you with?' She moved closer and tried not to breathe on his face as she spoke, 'Are you okay?' She reached out to touch his arm, but recoiled when it felt like she was about to put her hand inside a freezer.

'No, please don't worry yourself.' As if he was arthritic, he turned away and made his way through the living room towards the side door. The door opened by itself. Did the house want him to leave? He turned round and looked at her. 'Thank you for your time.' He took one last look around before he stepped outside.

From the doorstep, she watched as he made his way towards his car. The closer he got, the quicker he seemed able to move. He opened the driver's door, got into the car, slammed the door shut and drove away as if he was in hot pursuit.

As she looked across at *Diane*, she saw Peter and Lisa had company: a large black shadow and five smaller ones hovered beside them. She regarded them for a moment before she went back inside the house.

Eliza made her way down the stairs. 'Is everything okay?' She followed Mrs Caplin into the kitchen.

'I'm not sure, Eliza.' She picked up the empty wine bottle. 'Today keeps getting weirder; as though burying my daughter wasn't enough.' *Should I get myself another bottle from the cellar?* The hallucinations were hard to cope with and after the earlier telephone conversation with Robert, she decided against it. She put the bottle on top of the other empties in the recycling box.

*

Lisa looked up at the house. *That officer mustn't have been looking for me. Unless Mum told him I wasn't here, or she made up another excuse. But didn't he see me watching him? I thought he had; obviously not. He wouldn't have known who I was anyway. Maybe he wasn't here for me. Was he looking for Robert? I wonder what he's been up to.* She saw Elizabeth and Eliza looking out of the kitchen window and assumed they chatted about her.

*

'Why don't you take the rest of the day off, Eliza? Lisa's given Harry the day off, so it only seems fair. I should've said something earlier.' Elizabeth sensed something else was going to happen and thought it for the best that Eliza went home.

'That'd be great. Are you sure you'll be okay on your own? I don't mind staying with you if you need company.' Eliza did not point out her working day had almost finished. But there was another reason she could not leave: she had not had chance to explain about the damage she had done in the bedroom.

'I'm not going to have another drink if that's what you're worried about.'

'That's not what I meant,' Eliza said. 'Mrs Caplin … I lost my temper earlier and punched a hole in

97

your bedroom wall.' She took a deep breath. 'I've tried to clean up the mess, but I've made the blood stains on your carpet look worse.' She looked remorseful. 'I'm sorry. I'll pay for the damage. You could deduct the money from my wages.' Her confession had brought her relief, but she wondered why Mr Caplin, who must have seen the damage when he packed, had not questioned what had happened before he left.

'I know that's not what you meant, Eliza, but I'll be fine. We'll talk about the damage tomorrow.' She paused. 'Although, there is something I'd like your help with before you go home, if you don't mind.' She smiled. 'And I want you to make me a promise, when you get home, you'll make an appointment with your doctor.' She pointed at the cut on Eliza's hand. 'It might be a good idea if you call in at the hospital on your way home and get someone to look at that cut for you; get some proper stitches. The last thing you need is for it to get infected.'

Eliza looked at her seeping cut. She pressed on a couple of the butterfly stitches to stick them back down. 'I don't think I'll go to the hospital.' She scowled. 'I don't want to waste their time. Besides, they'll have proper sick people to care for. This is self-inflicted.' She held up her injured hand. 'Why should someone else have to sort it? Plus, I don't want to have to explain how I did it.' She put her hand down. 'Anyway, what do you need help with?'

*

Ten minutes later, the task was done, and they were back inside the house.

Elizabeth felt an overwhelming urge for Eliza to leave. She opened the side door. 'I'll see you in the morning, nice and early.' She folded her arms to stop herself from pushing Eliza outside.

A little perplexed, Eliza grabbed her jacket and draped it over her shoulders. 'I'll see you in the morning,' she said. *Why did Mrs Caplin need my help? She could have done the task by herself.*

From the doorstep, Elizabeth watched Eliza as she made her way down the drive.

The gate had opened slightly. Eliza squeezed through the gap and did not look back.

Before Elizabeth made her way back inside the house, she looked across at the shed door's padlock to check it was secure and then looked down at *Diane*. There was no sign of Lisa, Peter, or the black shadows.

She closed the side door behind her, leant her back against it, put her head back and sighed with relief.

From the kitchen, Lisa had heard the side door close and Elizabeth's audible breath. She turned her head from left to right as she examined her reflection in the window. The face that looked back at her did not resemble her usual appearance; the one everyone else saw every day. She had seen that guise before, many times. The vision had never scared her. Her complexion was a pale grey. Her eyes, with dilated pupils, had recessed within their sockets. She saw

Elizabeth look straight at her as she moved towards her. Could Elizabeth see what she saw? Elizabeth stopped a couple of feet behind her.

With no way back, Elizabeth knew she had to be strong. Fear oozed from her pores; could Lisa smell her?

The silence felt endless. Who would speak first?

'Is Peter still on the boat?' Elizabeth was surprised by how calm she sounded, and then wondered if Lisa was aware of the conversation that had taken place in the park.

Lisa continued to watch Elizabeth's reflection. 'Yes,' she said. She wondered why the shadows lingered. Protection for Peter? From what? Was he in danger?

'Will he be okay next to the water?' Elizabeth decided not to mention the black shadows.

'*Now* she's worried about my son's welfare.' Lisa turned round, raised her eyebrows, licked her chapped lips, and took a deep breath before she continued, 'He'll be fine. Do you think I'd leave him by himself if he weren't?'

Elizabeth did not dare to respond. What if she said the wrong thing? She thought about the quiet, little girl she once knew; the one who had liked to play alone.

'Did you mean what you said earlier?' The harshness in Lisa's tone remained.

'What about?' The surrounding walls appeared to edge closer. 'I'm not sure what I'm saying half of the time nowadays.'

'Do you wish it was me who was dead instead of Susan?' Lisa hoped she had misheard and needed confirmation.

A sudden movement, near the bottom of the stairs, caught Elizabeth's attention. She turned to check, but there was nothing there. 'Oh, Lisa, don't be silly. Of course, I don't wish you were dead.' If what Damian had told her was true, she could not show any signs of weakness, as Lisa had not had any trouble when she had killed the rest of their family, but would she do the same to her?

'Why did you say it then? How would you feel if I said I wish you weren't my mother?'

'I don't know.' Elizabeth looked at the floor. 'Like I said, I don't know what I'm saying half of the time.' She lifted her eyes. 'My mind's all over the place at the moment.' She paused. 'And yes, I'd be upset if you said that to me.'

Lisa had a hunch Elizabeth had meant what she had said. Would there be any point in repeating the conversation? The words had been said and could not be taken back. It was time to move on. 'Would you like me to cook us something nice for our dinner? I could go to the supermarket and get the ingredients for a Spaghetti Bolognaise.'

Elizabeth's stomach rumbled. She could not remember the last time she had had a proper meal; let alone one cooked by Lisa. 'That'd be lovely, thank you.'

'And then, when we're all seated around the table, you can tell me why that priest and Victoria Willis's

101

mother were here and where you went shortly after that.'

Unaware Lisa had seen Damian and Melanie, Elizabeth tried not to act surprised, but her eyes still widened.

'I didn't realise you knew Mrs Willis. Did she come all the way up here just to pass on her condolences? That's a long journey. Couldn't she have picked up the phone and rung you? If she found your address, I'm sure she could've found your phone number.'

'I guess, but I think they said something about being in the area anyway.' Elizabeth gulped. 'I thought it was thoughtful of them.'

'It was,' Lisa said. 'You see, Mum, there are nice people out there despite all the horrible stuff that keeps happening.'

Elizabeth smiled, but she was not ready to relax.

'But what about the priest? Who is he? I'm sure he's not from Beechwood. Do you know him?'

'No, he came along with Melanie to keep her company.'

'Are they a couple?' Lisa paused. 'Hang on, now I think about it, I think I've seen him before.' She nodded. 'He's an odd little creature, isn't he?'

Elizabeth thought it rude to talk about a man of the cloth in that way.

'Where did you go this afternoon? It's unusual for you to go out nowadays; especially by yourself. Me and Peter would have gone with you if you'd asked.'

'I went out for a walk,' Elizabeth said hastily. 'I needed to clear my head and be by myself for a while. I decided to go for a stroll around the park; I've not been for a while.' Her chest tightened. Was Lisa suspicious?

'It looked like you were going for more than a stroll. You looked like you were on a mission. Were you going to meet someone?'

'Who like?'

'Oh, I don't know, Mum; perhaps the priest and Mrs Willis for example.'

Elizabeth gulped. 'I did bump into them as I strolled around the lake.'

'What are the chances, eh? If I were the paranoid type, I'd think the rendezvous had been arranged and then I'd have to ask myself why they wanted to meet up with you away from here. What could they have to tell you that they couldn't have said when they were here earlier?'

A sudden chill made Elizabeth shiver. 'Nothing exciting.' She paused. 'We talked about the weather and the neighbourhood. I wasn't there for long.' She was aware she had been gone longer than it took to talk about the weather – which was usually wet – and the area – which was lakes, mountains, and ramblers.

'Not the first time you've lied, Mother,' Lisa muttered.

Elizabeth frowned. 'Pardon?'

'I said, they must be staying somewhere local.'

'I've no idea; I didn't ask.' Aware that was not what Lisa had said, Elizabeth thought it best to let the subject go.

'Anyway, I agree; it was kind of them to call round to see you.' Lisa pointed towards *Diane*. 'Peter doesn't want to go anywhere. I've told him he can stay on the boat until I get back. I'm sure he'll be fine, but could you keep an eye on him?'

'Yes.' Relieved the interrogation was over, Elizabeth's shoulders slumped.

'Do you need anything else while I'm out?'

'No, thank you.' Elizabeth smiled. She preferred the simpler questions where she only had to answer with a yes or a no.

Lisa made her way through the living room and exited through the side door. *What has that little worm said to my mother?* She would drive Susan's car to the supermarket. Was she insured? Did she care? That was the least of her problems.

Unaware Lisa had planned to take Susan's car, Elizabeth looked out of the kitchen window. She pictured Susan behind the steering wheel as the car moved towards the gate. For a moment, her heart felt complete again and she thought the sun shone brighter. Susan turned her head and looked up at her. Her face lit up as she waved. She looked like she did before her accident. But her smile soon turned to screams as flames engulfed her. Her face started to melt and stuck to the window as she tried, in vain, to open the door. Elizabeth heard her cries for help. But there was nothing she could do. She put her hands over her ears and shook her head.

A moment later, reality resumed.

Lisa looked straight ahead at the gate. The gate opened and she drove through.

Elizabeth looked towards *Diane*. Peter was nowhere in sight. The large black shadow was motionless while the small black shadows hovered over the jetty.

She opened the French doors, stepped outside, inhaled deeply, and made her way towards the lake. She stopped beside the willow and looked at the black shadows again. Might they harm her if she got closer? She waited a moment until she found the courage to continue.

The small black shadows moved aside and allowed her to pass. They turned as though watching her. Could they smell her fear? She climbed aboard *Diane* and looked across at Peter who was seated on a bench kicking his feet backwards and forwards. The large black shadow turned and watched as she moved towards him. An aroma grew stronger; the familiarity stirred memories. Where had she smelt it before? A cigar? The black shadow leant forward. Did it try to smell her or look closer at her?

'Hi, Grandma.' His mood had improved.

She leant forward and put her hand on his knee. 'Hi, Peter, are you okay?' She wondered if he could see the black shadows watching over him. If he could, he did not make it obvious as he never looked at them.

105

'I'm fine, Grandma.' He frowned and stuck out his bottom lip. 'Eliza was mean. She scared me.'

'Oh no, what did she do?' She hoped the incident in her bedroom, that Eliza had spoken of, had not involved him.

'She shouted.' He screwed up his face.

'Why? Were you naughty?'

'No.' He folded his arms. 'I was playing.'

She thought about how best to explain Eliza's situation. 'I don't think she's well. She's left for the day. I'll have a chat with her when she comes back tomorrow.' She put her hand on his cheek. 'I'll ask her to apologise; is that okay?'

He moved his head away from her touch. 'Okay.'

'Do you want to come back inside the house? We could play a board game, or I could read to you if you like.'

'No, thank you.' He looked up at the black shadow as if it was a cute puppy.

He can see it. Why isn't he afraid? 'Well, you be careful and give me a shout if you need anything.' She looked up at the black shadow and narrowed her eyes.

'I will.' He nodded.

She felt light-headed as she straightened up. She leant forward, grabbed her knees, and looked ahead.

Her light-headedness soon passed. She straightened up again, stretched out her arms and looked up at the black shadow again. *What is it? Why's it here?* At times it grew denser. Was it made from some type of gas? If she touched it, would she be able

106

to feel what it was made from, or would her hand go straight through? Although tempted, she resisted.

Peter watched as she alighted and made her way towards the house.

The landline rang. She made her way through the kitchen towards the living room. Her walk turned into a jog. She answered the telephone before the answering machine activated.

'Mrs Caplin?' It was unusual for Harry to call on the landline. He sounded concerned.

'Yes, Harry.' She gasped. 'Is everything okay?'

'I was checking to make sure everything was okay with you?'

'I'm fine.' She paused. 'Why do you ask?' She reached for her reliever. *Has Eliza spoken with him about our earlier conversation?*

He waited until she had finished with her reliever before he said, 'I'm sure it's nothing. Just me being a silly old man. I've got this niggling feeling something bad is going to happen and I can't seem to shake it off. Do you ever get those feelings, Mrs Caplin?'

'I do, Harry.'

'Would you like me to come over and keep you company until Mr Caplin gets back? I don't mind. To be honest it would put *my* mind at rest.'

'Thank you, Harry, that's kind of you, but I'll be fine. Don't forget, I've got Lisa and Peter to keep me company.' She was fond of him, but wondered how a sweet elderly man could protect her.

'Is everyone else, okay?'

'I think so; although it's been a strange kind of a day.' There was a click sound on the line, as though a third-party had listened in and then hung-up. 'Hello? What was that?'

He did not answer.

'Harry, are you there?' She pulled the handset from her ear and studied it. Had she expected it to melt?

Someone or something was on the line. She heard their raspy breathing. She kept quiet, listened, and waited a moment longer before she put down the handset.

With her hand poised over the telephone, she waited for it to ring again. When it did not, she picked up the handset and put it against her ear. A crackling sound lasted for several seconds before the usual tone returned. She opened the telephone table's drawer and got out a little black book that had everyone's contact details. She found Harry's mobile phone number and rang him. The call went through to voicemail. She decided not to leave a message, put the handset down and rang Lisa.

Lisa answered after two rings. She supported her mobile phone between her ear and shoulder. 'Mum, I'm at the checkout. Can you give me a second?' She took her change from the cashier and mimed her thanks. 'If there's something you've remembered you need, I can still grab it before I leave.'

In the background, enthusiastic checkout cashiers' tills beeped as they scanned barcodes.

'No, I don't need anything. I was just checking to make sure everything was okay.'

'I'm fine, Mum,' she said, although she had a pulsating headache and chronic indigestion. 'I'll be back soon.'

Elizabeth put down the handset. *I'm losing my mind. Everyone's right: I've been drinking too much and my imagination's running wild; especially the part where I'm seeing black shadows. And did I really see a priest and Melanie?* She looked at the telephone and wondered if Harry had tried to call back. *But Lisa saw them too. Why am I considering what they told me. I don't know him and only recognised her. Come on, the whole thing's ludicrous.*

The gate opened with an unusual sound; comparable to someone scraping their fingernails down a blackboard. She opened the side door and, from the doorstep, checked on who might be there. It could not have been Lisa because she would have had to have driven faster than the speed of light to get back so quick. Had she expected anyone else? She could not remember; her mind was foggy.

Robert's car stopped, askew, outside one of the outbuildings. Was it him behind the wheel though? He always liked to park straight and usually manoeuvred several times before he was satisfied. Too much in a hurry to care, Robert got out and slammed the door shut.

Relieved to see him, she rushed across to greet him.

He hurried past her without saying a word.

She pointed at the gate. 'You've left the gate open.'

He muttered something under his breath and continued towards the side door.

Four white vans, with three men inside each, drove through the gateway and parked randomly. Robert closed the gate.

Already aware he had not come back for her sake, she said, 'I wasn't expecting you back until tomorrow.' She followed him into the house.

'We need to get some stock shifted.' His manner was blasé.

He moved the oil painting, of their house, which hung over the fireplace, and propped it on the floor against the wall. Behind where the picture had hung, embedded in the wall, was a safe. He punched a combination of numbers on the keypad, turned the key, took out a large wad of banknotes and a bunch of keys.

She had been unaware of the safe. 'Is there anything I can help you with?'

Two of his men walked in and upturned the sofas.

'Can you mind out of the way.' Robert sighed. 'I don't want you to get knocked over.' He pushed her aside and hurried towards the door where four of his men waited. He passed a key to each of them and pointed, in turn, to different outbuildings. 'You all know what needs to be done; you know the drill.'

She leant her back against the wall, beside the fireplace, and watched the two men unzip the compartments under the sofas. They pulled out shiny white building blocks, which were smaller than your average house brick, and piled them on the floor.

Robert returned to help. Like a go-between, he picked up an armful of blocks and carried them to another man on the doorstep.

As she surveyed the room, she wondered if there was anything else hidden away inside the house, perhaps behind the bath panel, underneath the floorboards or inside a secret room? 'A policeman called earlier looking for you,' she said.

'Yes, I know.' He did not turn to look at her. 'That officer's a good mate of mine. I've known him since he was a lad.'

She surmised what the officer had wanted with Robert. Was he corrupt? She had seen his sort in the movies, but did they exist in real life? Was he on Robert's payroll? Had he called to warn him about a raid? 'Did your police friend call for anything official? You're not in any trouble? He just made a social call, did he?' She wanted to scream at him and get him to answer, but she kept calm. Would he have told her the truth anyway?

He continued with the task in hand before he said, 'Don't worry.' He made his way towards her. She expected him to pat her head as if she was an obedient dog, but he hugged her – briefly.

She thought about Peter as she made her way towards the door. *I'd better go and check on him. He's probably wondering what all these men are doing here.* But she remembered he was contented when she last saw him, and he was not alone; he had the black shadows to keep him company. *He doesn't need me either.* She made her way up the stairs, rested half-way, and continued to watch the cocaine removal operation. *I wonder what the street value is.*

Robert's men worked quickly and methodically as they emptied the outbuildings. Hours of planning had gone on before in case of such an emergency. The vans were loaded with stolen goods, counterfeit items, and the outbuilding – which held a fake documentation workshop – was emptied.

Chapter Ten

The Stand-Off

The siren drew closer. Lisa checked her speedometer, glanced in the rear-view mirror, and saw the police car's flashing blue lights. Did Susan's car have a faulty light? She had not checked before she had driven off.

She signalled left and pulled into the side of the road. The police car overtook, did not slow down or pull in. *Come on, why would the police be concerned about me or a couple of damaged cars? Surely, they've got more serious crimes to deal with, like murders or armed robberies.* She checked her mirrors, signalled, and pulled out.

She was unaware Robert had arranged for her car to be collected and sent to the crusher. The police had no idea her car had been involved in an incident and the dog walker's mobile phone, which had photographic evidence of her trashed car, was damaged beyond repair.

The police car slowed down. She caught up to it. It turned on to Caplin Lane. *Uh-oh, I knew the police were looking for me!* She thought about driving on. *Of course, they won't know what I look like or who's driving this car.* She decided to signal and followed them. She had to face the consequences of her actions and she did not want Peter to worry about where she was.

She pulled up behind the police car. Its siren and flashing lights had stopped. She switched off her engine.

The four officers in the car continued to stare ahead.

She waited a moment longer and considered what to do next. Why had they driven fast to just sit and wait? With the key still in the ignition, she got out, left her door ajar and made her way towards the gate.

With her finger poised, mid-air, about to press the intercom button, she stopped when she heard a car door open behind her.

An officer got out of the front passenger seat and slammed his door shut.

She lowered her arm and listened to his footsteps as he made his way towards the boot of the car.

He took out a semi-automatic rifle, made his way towards her and stopped a couple of feet behind. The two back-seat officers got out and made their way towards the boot.

She turned round and squinted; it was difficult to see his face as the sun was behind him. She shielded her eyes, saw his rifle, bulletproof vest, and his pistol in his holster. She looked across at the other officers who were also armed. *Wow, what a lot of weapons. Well, at least, I know they're not here for me. But why are they here?*

'Excuse me, miss. Do you live here?' the officer said.

She nodded.

'Is Mr Caplin at home?'

So, it's Robert who's been a naughty boy. 'No, he's away on business. Can I help you?' She raised an eyebrow. For a moment, she forgot about her headache and indigestion.

'Could you open the gate, miss?' With a poker face, he continued to look at her. 'We'd like to take a look for ourselves.'

Don't they need a warrant or something? She shrugged, turned round, and pressed the intercom button. 'Mum, it's me. Can you open the gate?' She was curious as to what the police wanted with Robert but did not probe further. What did she care? They were not there for her.

Elizabeth, who had not checked the intercom's monitor, was unaware Lisa was not alone.

The gate opened. Three officers strolled through the gateway. Lisa made her way back towards Susan's car. The police car edged forward. She glanced at the driver's face, but he stared ahead.

When she got back to the car, she saw her gaunt reflection in the driver's window: a grey complexion, sunken eyes, and dilated pupils. No one else seemed horrified by her appearance. Was she the only one who could see what she looked like?

She drove through the gateway and parked beside the police car at the bottom of the drive. The gate stayed open. Shocked by the chaos, she looked in-between the vans and tried to work out what was happening. She saw Robert's car parked up outside one of the outhouses but did not recognise any of the men who scurried about. She decided to avoid whatever was going on, left the Spaghetti Bolognaise ingredients strewn on the back seat and went to check on Peter.

With his chin rested on the back of his hand, Peter peered over the side of *Diane*. He saw Mummy approach and waved at her.

The small black shadows continued to hover over the jetty while the large black shadow watched over him.

She boarded, made her way towards him, and stood beside him. 'Did I miss anything?'

He turned his head, looked up at her and tried to smile: a pitiful attempt. He knew something bad, that made him feel sad, but he was not allowed to tell.

'Are you okay?' She put her hand under his chin and lifted his head.

He tried to nod, but her hand prevented it.

'I was worried earlier when you wouldn't speak to me.' She moved her hand from his chin. 'If there's anything you want to talk about, I'm here for you. Okay?' She ruffled his hair. 'Anything at all.' She smiled.

He nodded again, turned his head, and watched the chaos continue.

At the bottom of the drive, the outnumbered officers had positioned themselves strategically; each of them ready to open fire on Robert or any of his accomplices.

Robert put his hands above his head. 'You got me.' He smirked.

Lisa watched. *He knew the police were coming for him and they knew he knew.* She wondered if any of the officers had spoken. *What were his men loading into those vans? What's he involved in?* She smiled. *I always knew he was dodgy.* She knelt beside Peter and put her arm around his shoulders.

With her hand over her mouth, Elizabeth watched from the doorstep. She could not believe what she was seeing. The scene reminded her of a 1980's television drama.

An unexpected gunshot echoed. Bernard, one of Robert's men, had got jumpy and his trembling finger pulled the trigger.

The shot hit an officer. The bullet gouged his jugular. Blood spurted from him like a burst waterpipe. He was dead within seconds.

Elizabeth screamed, put her hands over her ears, ran back inside the house and did not stop until she reached the kitchen.

Lisa and Peter ducked.

Another shot fired.

In real-time, only a short time had passed, but it felt more like hours before Lisa dared to straighten up again to check on what had happened. She saw the officer, who she had spoken with, laid in a pool of blood. She scanned the drive. Another man was down. Bernard was on the ground, propped against an outbuilding, with a bullet hole in the centre of his forehead. The exit wound was not visible, but the bullet had obviously travelled through his head as morsels of his brain were splattered on the wall; a crimson pattern slid towards the ground.

No longer smug, Robert lowered his weary arms. His right hand twitched as he yearned to grab the pistol that was tucked in the back of his belt. How many of his men carried weapons? He realised he should have known. Although his men outnumbered the officers, resistance was futile if only a couple of his men were armed.

Lisa looked up at the house. She saw Elizabeth through the kitchen window. *That officer must have called earlier to warn Robert about the raid. He must have rung him on his mobile phone. How else would Robert have known the police were coming? He got away from his meeting and got back here quick enough.*

Robert raised his hands again, stepped forward, looked towards the gate, and started to walk down the drive.

The side door was still open. Charles, another of Robert's men, jumped out of the back of a van and ran inside the house.

Lisa watched as Elizabeth turned her head to look at Charles, opened her mouth, and screamed.

Robert showed no concern as he listened to Elizabeth's cries for help; although, he did stop for a moment to put his hands behind his head before he continued towards the officers. 'It's me you're after.' He tilted his head to one side and then the other. 'Let my men go and I give you my word I'll come peacefully.'

The officers remained poised to shoot.

Lisa looked up at the black shadow.

The black shadow moved towards the jetty. It hovered for a moment beside the small black shadows before it manoeuvred unnoticed, close to the ground, alongside the rose bushes and up towards the house. It drifted through the wall of the house and stopped beside Elizabeth.

'If you shut up with your damn screaming, I won't be forced to hurt you,' Charles said through gritted teeth. He considered if his behaviour towards the boss's wife was worth the punishment.

She stopped screaming, but her mouth stayed open and not because of Charles's threat.

The black shadow had wrapped itself around Charles, like a black veil, and then it possessed his body.

Charles looked drained of energy; like he might collapse. His pale complexion emphasised his dilated pupils within darkened sockets. He regarded how alarmed she looked. His lips parted to speak, but no words came out. His body shivered. He rose several feet, laid horizontally and rotated as if he was skewered over a fire. After several turns, he stopped and floated out of the kitchen, through the living room and up the stairs.

What would happen to him next? Out of curiosity, she wanted to follow, but her instincts warned her to stay where she was.

*

'Get down on the ground and put your hands out to the sides,' one of the officers shouted.

A stone jabbed Robert's left knee as he fell to the ground. He lowered himself until he was laid on his stomach; his pistol was exposed.

*

119

The black shadow, who still had Charles in its grasp, was in a spare bedroom.

Charles had soiled his trousers, front and back. His stomach made churning noises. He and the black shadow circled the room a while longer, up and down, round and round, faster and faster, before they flew towards the window.

Charles, who was unable to shield his head with his arms, and the black shadow flew through the pane.

The sound of breaking glass made everyone outside turn their heads to look. Shards exploded over the lawn.

Charles felt slashes across his skin. He did not fall to the ground straightaway. Instead, he gained height. He hovered mid-air, for a moment, and then plunged as if he had fallen from an aeroplane.

The black shadow returned to *Diane*.

Elizabeth opened the French doors and ran outside. She looked across at Charles's lifeless body, laid beside the willow, and then up at the broken window before she rushed back inside. *When will this nightmare end?*

*

'Are you okay, Peter?' Lisa knew everything that was going on should have been too much for a child to see.

He did not answer.

'If you want, we can take Auntie Susan's car, get out of here and come back when all this is over.'

120

'I'm okay, Mummy.' His attention reverted to the carnage. He wondered if a goody or a baddy would be hurt next.

Unsure if she should allow him to make that type of decision for himself, she thought he seemed happy and said, 'Well, if, you're sure.'

Damian and Melanie sauntered through the gateway. As they made their way past the stand-off, something caught her attention. She turned her head to check on what glistened and saw sunlight reflect from a sliver of glass. She noticed other shards of glass and a bloodied twisted corpse. Aghast, she looked up at the broken window and knew the man must have been pushed. Had Damian noticed? Without a reaction or a sound, she glanced at him. She was unsure. He never gave much away.

Lisa narrowed her eyes when she saw them near the top of the drive. 'What the *fuck* are they doing here?' she muttered.

Peter smirked; he had heard what she said.

The side door was still open. Damian stepped on to the doorstep and leant through the doorway. He peered inside the house and knocked twice before he studied the floor in front of him; his unperturbed manner suggested all was quiet outside.

Melanie checked over her shoulder for any stray bullets headed her way and for any bodies flying out of any of the upstairs windows.

*

Still face down on the ground with his hands cuffed behind him, Robert's pistol was gone.

His men had hidden. Some had taken cover, crouched inside their vans, underneath their dashboards. Others tried to hide behind their vans, but still in plain sight with their feet visible. They kept peeking to check if it was clear to come out.

He paid them generously for their time but had given no instructions on what to do should they get caught. Should they run or surrender?

*

Elizabeth had heard the knocks on the side door. She felt apprehensive as she made her way to answer and was not surprised to see Damian and Melanie on the doorstep. 'Come in.' She gestured. 'I'm sorry about the commotion.' She hurried back towards the kitchen. He followed. Melanie hesitated in the doorway and turned to look at the man, with a bullet hole in his head, before she entered and closed the door behind her.

*

A police van with four officers arrived and parked at the bottom of the drive.

So, the rumours are true, Robert is the big-time gangster everyone loves to talk about. Lisa was unsure if she should feel impressed by his audacity or angry because he had dragged her mother into his world. Did Elizabeth know how he made his money?

The officers clambered out of the van and strutted towards Robert. Two of them grabbed an arm each and hauled him to his feet while the other two stood either side, on hand, in case he tried to make a run for freedom.

Robert grimaced and moaned.

Impressed with his associates, Lisa smiled and nodded. *He made that look too easy for them. He didn't even try to put up a fight. I bet there's someone high up in the force on his payroll. They'll probably let him off with a slap on the wrist and he'll be back home in time for supper.*

He continued to scowl and put up no resistance as the officers dragged him towards their van.

As they reached the van, one of the officers, who was stood beside him, rushed ahead to open the back door and the inner cage door. The other officer removed Robert's handcuffs.

Robert hunched over as he was shoved inside the van. His knees took the brunt of his fall. He winced and remained on the floor.

His men thought it pointless to hide any longer as the officers knew where they were. They reappeared, one by one; some with their hands above their heads. Two of them put their pistols on the ground; hopeful the police might be lenient with them.

With Robert locked inside the van, the four officers stood behind the armed officers. They evaluated the ongoing situation and realised they did not have enough vehicles to take them all into custody.

Meanwhile, his men realised they should have stayed hidden because despite their lack of weapons, they still outnumbered the officers. Perhaps if they had devised some type of distraction, a couple of them might have had chance to escape.

They watched the gate close. It was not a supernatural phenomenon. After a certain length of time, if the sensors were not triggered, the gate closed automatically.

None of the officers turned to look.

*

'Will you be okay if I leave you for a little while? I won't be long,' Lisa said to Peter. She needed to get up to the house to check on Elizabeth and to see what the priest had told her.

'Yes.'

She looked up at the black shadow and then back at Peter. The black shadow moved closer. She felt a sharp pain in her stomach. Although she wanted to wince, instead she feigned a smile.

She alighted, made her way along the jetty and up towards the house. Her stomach ache had worsened and made it difficult to walk upright. She presumed her trapped wind would pass and tried to ignore the cramps. She stopped beside the willow and took a closer look at Charles's shredded face. She tilted her head to one side and said, 'Ouch. Did you hurt yourself?' She sniggered as she made her way towards the French doors.

As she peered through the doors, she saw Elizabeth making drinks for Damian and Melanie. They had their backs to her.

*

The police van's back door opened; a gradual movement to start with as if Robert peeked out. The door was motionless for several seconds before it flew open as if he had kicked it with force; however, the inner cage door was still closed. Robert, who was still seated on a side bench, leant forward. He got to his feet, stooped forward and shuffled towards the door. The outer door lock was broken, and its hinges were bent. He peered out. No one was nearby.

Lisa turned round to check on where the noise came from. She made her way back towards the willow. As she stood beside the tree, her eyes were drawn towards Peter. She could not be certain from where she stood, but he seemed to frown in Robert's direction as though he concentrated hard.

The French doors opened. Muffled voices followed. Damian, Melanie, and Elizabeth made their way outside.

Damian's face remained void of emotion. Lisa was impressed by his priest impersonation. No wonder his intended victims always fell for his confident manner.

Melanie was apprehensive. Why wouldn't she be? Did she wonder how she had got herself into such a bizarre situation? Was she aware of what Damian was or what he could do? Lisa knew he would have introduced himself to Melanie while she felt alone and vulnerable. He would have pretended he was the perfect gentleman, turned on the charm, and once she had fallen into his trap, he would have offered her some of his wisdom.

*

Without instruction, in unison, the three officers laid down their rifles. Like programmed robots, they got to their feet, turned round, and made their way towards the gate. They took off their protective gear and discarded it in a heap. Side by side, they faced the gate and pressed their hands against it. The other officers copied; two to each side.

Robert's men looked at each other. They shrugged and frowned, but none of them asked the question.

*

'What's happening?' Elizabeth said to Lisa.

Lisa shook her head; although, she had an idea who would know.

Her stomach pain lingered. She had started to worry. What if it was more serious than flatulence? The last time she endured such pain was when she got food poisoning after a dodgy takeaway. She was convinced she was dying from dysentery; the diarrhoea had lasted for three days.

Something was stuck in the back of her throat. She put her hand over her mouth and coughed several times to try to dislodge whatever was there. Her head pounded. A lump of bloodied phlegm flew out and stuck, like glue, to her palm. She wiped it down the tree trunk.

*

The small black shadows moved away from the jetty and hovered beside Robert's men. Four of the shadows picked a man each and occupied their bodies while the other kept watch. They needed to practice the art of possession because one day one of them would become Peter's guardian. The other four would become guardians to his child and grandchildren.

The police van's inner cage door opened. A moment later, Robert looked out of the doorway. Unable to believe his luck, he checked around and jumped out. He rubbed his arms and stretched them out to his sides. He leant forward, rubbed his bruised knees and looked towards the gate at the officers who were grouped together. He had no idea what was happening. He turned his head to look at his men. All, but four, looked terrified.

*

'You've got to stop them,' Damian said to Lisa.

Lisa made her way towards the drive.

Melanie, who continued to bite her fingernails, turned round and walked back into the kitchen where she felt safer. She wanted no part of what was about to happen. That was not the reason she was there. The deal had been to get him inside Elizabeth's house to enable him to get to Lisa and then she would be rewarded.

Elizabeth followed her.

'Now will you believe me?' he said and then hurried inside.

'I still don't see what any of this proves. You've told me Lisa's a demon, but these officers aren't here for my daughter, they're here for Robert and his men. My husband's the one who's done wrong, not her.'

Melanie looked at him. 'I want to leave,' she said. 'I've changed my mind. I no longer want to be any part of this.'

He did not respond until she dashed towards the side door. For a second, his human guise faltered, and the winged entity appeared. 'You cannot leave,' he called after her.

She did not see his brief transformation.

But Elizabeth saw him for what he was. *He's the demon.* She had to be strong and show no weakness. 'Why can't Melanie leave? She's not a prisoner. She's free to leave whenever she wants.'

Melanie stopped beside the door and turned round. She felt a need to explain her decision further: 'All of this,' she waved her arms around to demonstrate, 'is too surreal. I'd already come to terms with Vicky's death and even though I miss her, I know I always will. It took me a long time to come to that realisation, but I think it's for the best if I allow her to rest in peace. At the time, it seemed like a good idea to come here, but I don't need to do any of this. I know, when my time ends, I'll see her again.'

Even though Elizabeth had no idea what Melanie referred to, she still smiled. She looked across at his drink. He had not touched it or the biscuits she had put on a plate for him. 'Aren't you going to have your drink, Damian?'

'Please do not go, Mel.' He furrowed his brow. 'We need to sit and think about what to do next for the best.' He did not raise his voice. He sounded like he did on that day when they first met at Beechwood train station.

She strolled back towards the kitchen, sat down beside him and looked underneath the table at the fire engine and the police car up against a table leg. She nudged them with her foot. 'I think you're mistaken.' She looked at him before she continued, 'Yes, this family's had more than its share of problems, but you tell me a family that hasn't.' She paused. 'But this talk of demons is utter nonsense. I'm not sure what you want from me, but whatever it is, I don't think I'm the one to help you.' She paused again. 'And even though it pains me to say it, I will forfeit my reward.'

Elizabeth made her way towards the window and looked out at the lake. She knew as she took a deep breath and closed her eyes, the image of Susan's charred body would still be clear in her mind.

*

Lisa stood between two rose bushes and watched four of Robert's men pick up a rifle each and aim them at the officers. *They're going to shoot.* She looked across at Peter who still watched the chaos unfold with the enthusiasm of a child who watched their favourite television programme. *It's Peter who's controlling the situation. But why? What have those men ever done to him?*

Robert's other men, who did not hold rifles, watched on, clueless and wide-eyed.

A sailboat, owned by one of Harry's friends, arrived at the jetty. Eliza and Harry alighted.

Both had the same sense of impending tragedy as they watched the boat pull away. They waved his friend off and turned round to look up at the house. Several times, they had tried to call Mrs Caplin on her

129

landline and on her mobile phone but were always greeted with an engaged tone or a continuous buzzing sound.

Lisa had heard the boat arrive. She made her way across to investigate, but the sound of gunfire stopped her. She ducked, closed her eyes, and wrapped her arms over her head.

Five shots were fired. One accidentally; that bullet had gone astray. It was not enough to kill every officer. Had his men decided to pick officers at random? Would they kill the others? If so, when?

But none of the officers had been shot. For some unknown reason, his men had changed their target at the last second. Four bullets had hit Robert: one was lodged in his head; another had ripped open his throat and two had pierced his heart. He was dead before he hit the ground.

Lisa opened her eyes, moved her arms from over her head and straightened up. She looked around and saw Robert on the ground. *What the* ... It took her a moment longer to work out what had happened. Her eyes widened. She turned and ran towards *Diane*. She had to stop Peter before he made anything else happen.

Elizabeth ran through the house and opened the side door. When she heard the gunfire, she knew it was Robert who was dead from the unexplainable feeling in the pit of her stomach. Cautiously, she leant through the doorway and peered down the drive, but the vehicles blocked her view. Everyone moved in slow motion and any noise sounded muffled. Seconds later, normality resumed, everyone dashed around, and the noise got louder.

She heard someone screaming. She looked around. A moment later, she realised it was her. She was stood beside his body and had no recollection of how she had got there.

*

Melanie jumped to her feet.

Damian reached out, as though to touch her arm, and said, 'Stay here. *Please*. Do not go outside.' If she went outside to investigate, she would try to leave, and he needed her to stay, so they would allow him to stay. He withdrew his hand.

*

Harry and Eliza were already on *Diane* when Lisa climbed aboard.

'What's going on?' Harry said.

Lisa caught a glimpse of her grandparents' souls, Fred and Katherine Hurst, before they vanished. She frowned. *Why were they here?*

Peter got up from the deck, rubbed his elbow and climbed back up on to the bench. Had he fallen or was he pushed? There was a bullet hole where he had previously been seated.

Lisa stared at the hole. *They were here to save his life. They must have pushed him out of the way.*

'The police are here about Mr Caplin's drugs, aren't they?' Eliza said.

Harry and Lisa turned to look at her. 'What drugs?' he said.

Lisa's head pulsated like someone practiced the drums against her temples. Every inch of her body ached. Did she have influenza? 'You knew there were drugs in the house?' She covered her mouth in time to catch a cough. Bloodied spittle landed on her palm. She put her hand inside her pocket and wrapped it around a tissue. 'My son could have found them.' Unsure if Peter had heard, she looked across at him.

He continued to watch the chaos he had helped to create.

'I'm sorry.' Eliza paused. 'I thought everyone knew what Mr Caplin got up to. It's common knowledge around here. Everyone talks about him.'

Lisa knew Eliza was blameless. She knew the drugs had nothing to do with her. But why had she never heard the rumours herself? She had always suspected there was something underhand about him, which she had always chosen to ignore. 'Four of Robert's men have just killed him.'

'Why?' Eliza said.

How could Lisa begin to explain that most of what had happened was down to Peter? The simple answer was, she couldn't.

Peter looked at them out of the corner of his eye.

*

The four small black shadows withdrew from Robert's men.

The men looked down at the rifles they still clutched. They looked across at Robert's body and then at each other in search of an explanation.

His other men had taken cover, huddled in the back of a van, while the officers remained motionless against the gate.

Elizabeth, who no longer screamed, looked at the four men, as she tried to make sense of what had happened. Why had they shot her husband? She looked down at his mutilated body. It would have been pointless to try to resuscitate him. The realisation she had lost him forever hit her like a high-speed train. She felt cold, yet sweaty, and her teeth tingled. She clutched her stomach, doubled over and vomited.

*

Would it be hypocritical for Lisa to try to stop Peter? 'Are you okay?' she said before she looked up at the house.

He did not look at her as he nodded.

She did not ask the question, which was at the forefront of her mind, and instead she said, 'Do you want to talk about anything?' She brushed his fringe away from his eyes with her fingertips. Did he know what she referred to? Would he be able to give her a plausible explanation of why he had had Robert gunned down? Did he know what he had done or what he was capable of? Did he think he was just a little boy who liked to stretch his imagination while he played?

He shook his head.

She decided to drop the subject but would keep a close eye on him. 'I'm going to see if your grandma is all right. Will you be okay with Harry and Eliza?'

He nodded.

Harry, Eliza, and Peter watched Lisa as she made her way towards the drive.

Lisa stopped on the lawn, doubled over, pressed one hand against her chest and the other against her stomach. A moment later, she pulled herself together and straightened up.

Peter frowned. *What's wrong with Mummy?* She rarely got ill and when she did no one knew because she continued regardless.

'Were you hiding on the boat all along, Peter?' Eliza said. 'Did Mummy know where you were? Did she leave you by yourself?' Her smirk faded because if that was the case, why had Lisa tried to kill her?

He looked up at the black shadow before he looked at Eliza and raised his eyebrow. 'I wasn't by myself.'

Eliza and Harry looked at each other; aware of what the other thought.

*

'Mum?' Lisa felt partly to blame for what had happened, but how could she even begin to explain? Would Elizabeth believe her? If she did, what would she think of her and Peter?

Deep in thought, Elizabeth was taken by surprise. She had not seen or heard Lisa approach.

Lisa looked at the ground. Most of the vomit had soaked in, but the strong smell of alcohol lingered. 'Are you okay?' She noticed Elizabeth appeared to have aged ten years in a matter of minutes with greyer hair and deeper wrinkles.

Elizabeth's hand shook as she pointed down at Robert's body. Was it from shock, alcohol withdrawal, or both?

'I know.' Lisa put her hand on Elizabeth's shoulder and encouraged her to move away. With their heads bowed, they made their way up towards the house.

Lisa noted the empty unzipped compartments under the upturned sofas as she closed the side door behind them. She knew what would have been concealed inside.

When they made their way into the kitchen, they noticed neither Melanie nor Damian had moved.

'What's happened?' Melanie said.

'Robert's dead,' Lisa said.

Elizabeth burst into tears.

Melanie knew how Elizabeth felt. She rushed across to comfort her.

Lisa wished she had chosen her words more wisely or kept quiet. She noticed a copy of The Beechwood Chronicle on the table. Why was it there? Had Melanie and Damian brought it? The front headline read: ***Three Local Teenagers' Bodies Finally Found***. She had not been aware anyone was missing. Their photographs and names were stated underneath: ***Andrew, Adam, and Michael***. Their faces looked familiar, but she could not place them. Part of the article read: ***A walking stick was found leaning against a tree beside their shallow graves with a Royal Navy beret on top. The beret had belonged to a local named Frank; now deceased.***

His photograph was shown. *Is this man also responsible for other unsolved murders in the area?*

Damian looked away when Lisa caught him staring at her. She stared back. She liked to watch him squirm, but why was he there?

*

Peter surveyed Auntie Susan's car and then tried to use his telekinesis ability to move it. He had struggled for several minutes because he had got distracted a few times. He had only ever been able to move small objects. With his palms pressed against his ears, and his elbows rested on the side, he stared through the front passenger door as if it was transparent. The game proved much harder than he imagined, but at last the car rolled backwards. He wanted to cheer, but the exertion had made him feel weary. Sweat beads rolled down his forehead. His temporal veins bulged. Droplets of blood from his nose turned into a steady flow. Unperturbed, he leant over the side and his nosebleed trickled into the lake.

*

After careful consideration, Robert's men reappeared and joined the others who had shot him. They gawked at Susan's car, the police van, and the police car as they rolled down the drive and crushed the officers against the gate.

*

Inside the house, they seemed unaware the situation had worsened outside. As they were seated around the kitchen table, Damian's attention shifted between

Elizabeth and Melanie. He ignored Lisa, who watched him through narrowed eyes. 'We need to act before anyone else is killed,' he said.

Melanie and Elizabeth turned to look at him. Melanie's eyes widened and her mouth opened.

Lisa got up and rummaged through the drawer for painkillers. She popped two from a blister pack and swallowed them with a mouthful of water from the cold-water tap. *If this pain in my chest and stomach doesn't subside in the next half hour, I'll have to take a couple more.* She looked across at *Diane* through the kitchen window.

The black shadow looked up at her and waited.

She nodded once.

It moved away from Peter and stopped on the jetty for a moment before it made its way up towards the house. The small black shadows shifted positions. Two moved on to *Diane*, beside him, and the other three stayed on the jetty, spread equally apart.

She turned round and pointed to the living room mirror. 'You might want to check on your reflection,' she said to Damian.

He leapt up and examined himself. He had transformed into the winged entity and despite his best efforts, he did not seem able to change back into the priest.

Melanie and Elizabeth got to their feet. Their chairs fell back and crashed to the floor. Neither of them took their eyes off the hovering winged entity. How could such a well-spoken gentleman, and an apparent man of the cloth, be such a hideous-looking monster?

Elizabeth reached sideways and fumbled for Melanie's arm. They still stared as they stepped back and almost stumbled over their chairs.

The black shadow appeared in the room. Melanie was the only one who could not see it.

'Don't be scared,' Lisa said as she escorted Melanie and Elizabeth to the bottom of the stairs. 'This demon's not as bad as it looks.'

Chapter Eleven

More Bloodshed at the Caplin Residence

The local police station had lost contact with their colleagues. They presumed faulty equipment was to blame and sent another two officers along to investigate.

Officer Dobson and Officer Spencer were about to turn on to Caplin Lane. A group of wary neighbours, who had congregated at the end, moved aside to allow the police van to pass. The neighbours had heard gunshots and discussed if to call the police or try to investigate what had happened themselves.

Dobson slowed the van to a snail pace and lowered his window.

The neighbours looked inside the van.

Although the officer had noted their furrowed brows, he continued along the lane, pulled up outside the gate and switched off the engine. Both officers noted the eerie silence and looked at each other. Neither had any idea of the horror that awaited them on the other side.

Spencer, who was overweight and slow on his feet, opened the passenger door and got out, lakeside. As soon as his feet touched the ground, he overbalanced and almost fell forward. He had been in the police force since he left school. His best years were behind him. He believed humans could commit horrendous atrocities and was confident he had seen everything possible. There was nothing left to shock him. He left his door ajar, walked in front of the van and made his way towards the gate. He did not try to gain entry. Instead, he put his hands on his hips and stared at the gate for a moment as if he could see through the metal. *Why would a residential property need such a large barrier?*

Dobson, who was still young, had not seen much action. He remained seated. His hands gripped the steering wheel. He looked more like a getaway driver than an officer of the law. He checked his mirrors and then looked across at his colleague.

The designated spokesperson from the group of neighbours tried to run down the lane. Her stilettos made her teeter every few steps. 'We heard gunfire.' It was difficult to work out if she was posh or feigned a well-to-do accent.

The rest of the group edged closer and tried to look inconspicuous.

Concerned about the situation, Spencer knew all the officers involved with the assignment on a personal level and their immediate families. He stepped away from the gate, turned round and looked at her. He waited until she was nearer and said, 'Do you think the gunfire came from in here?' He pointed at the gate.

She looked back at the group who were too far away to have heard what he had said. With faces void of emotion, they stayed still as if they were in the middle of a game of musical statues. She turned back round, looked at him and said, 'We're not sure.' She felt like a busybody, smiled coyly and shrugged.

He turned round to press the intercom button, but a niggling doubt made his finger stop mid-air. He made his way back towards the van and stopped beside Dobson's window. 'Can you check to see if we can get access to this property via the lake? We should be able to. Radio in, will you? But warn them they *must* approach with extreme caution.'

Dobson nodded and reached for the radio.

As Spencer made his way back towards the gate, he wondered how many casualties there might be. 'How many shots did you hear?' he said.

'Sorry, I'm not sure.' She shook her head. Her face reddened. She had no creditable information to give him. 'There was one … then another … and a little later a few more. I didn't think to count at the time.'

'How long ago did you hear the gunshots?'

'Sorry, I didn't notice what the time was.' She shook her head again. She needed backup and turned her head to look at the group. 'Any idea of how many shots were fired or how long ago?' Her voice tapered off, aware whoever was on the other side of the gate might hear.

The group looked at each other and waited for someone else to answer.

Obvious none of them had any idea either, and no one had mentioned any of these details earlier, she turned to face the officer and shrugged again.

*

Elizabeth was racked with guilt as she climbed the stairs. For the first time in weeks, her next drink was the last thing on her mind.

Melanie had climbed the stairs ahead of her. 'What is that thing?' she said.

'Nothing for you to worry about,' Lisa said. 'As I said before, it looks a lot worse than it is.' She coughed. Her mouth filled with the taste of metallic blood. She swallowed.

Elizabeth stopped, grabbed the handrail, and turned to look at her. 'But what are *you* going to do? What can you do?' She shook her head. *What's going on?* She pointed towards the kitchen. 'Damian … I mean that thing, told me you're a demon.' She frowned. 'What did he mean? Are you possessed? We can get you help; whatever you need.'

Lisa's laugh turned into a grimace. The painkillers, she had taken earlier, had not dulled her pain. She needed to take more, but it would have to wait. Damian was her priority. 'No, I'm not possessed. Do I look like a demon to you?' She gestured before she pointed at the winged entity hovering beside the black shadow. 'Wouldn't you say he's the one who looks more like a demon?'

The light inside the house had darkened and made it feel more like the middle of the night. The temperature plummeted and made it feel more like a harsh winter.

Unsure which of the two creatures Lisa referred to, Elizabeth shrugged. *What's a demon supposed to look like?* As far as she knew he had not harmed anyone, but his appearance gave the impression he was a demon. *He's got wings though. Doesn't that mean he's an angel? Could he be a good demon? Is there such a creature?*

142

She was unaware he also collected souls and had used Melanie and Eliza to get to Lisa.

'I realise it was a long time ago, Mum, but don't you remember giving birth to me? Or do you think you brought the wrong baby home from hospital?'

'But I don't understand what *you* can do to get it out of my home.' Elizabeth's eyes welled up.

'I'm going to ask it to leave.' Lisa gestured for her to continue up the stairs. 'Simple as that.'

'And if he doesn't listen, what will you do then?'

'He will.' Lisa paused. 'I won't give him a choice.'

With nothing else for Elizabeth to say, she continued up the stairs and joined Melanie who waited at the top. The pair made their way along the landing towards the master bedroom.

Lisa waited a moment longer until they were out of sight. When she was confident, they would not be overheard, she made her way towards the kitchen.

*

'What's going on? We've got to get out of here,' Milton, one of Robert's men, said. He looked towards the lake and started to run.

Justin, another of his men, picked up a rifle from the ground, aimed it at Milton and shouted, 'Did you shoot Robert?'

Milton slowed down and turned his head. With a look of bewilderment, he mumbled, 'No … I don't know.' He tripped, put his hands out in front of him, and fell on a rose bush. The thorny stem snapped. A long thin spike pierced his right palm. Several other spikes ripped through his trousers and cut into his skin.

Austin, another of his men, stepped forward. Deep frown lines ran the length of his forehead. He pointed at Justin and Milton. 'It was both of you.' He spat on the ground and pointed at the other two offenders: Kyle and Leo. 'Why did any of you shoot him?'

Justin crouched, put the weapon on the ground and then ran towards the lake. Milton scrambled to his feet and ran in the same direction. Kyle and Leo followed. The others watched on.

*

Peter, who appeared weary, turned his head and looked at the small black shadows. 'Go,' he said. 'I'll be okay.' His nose bleed had stopped. He had bloodied streaks down his chin and across his cheek from where he had wiped the back of his hand under his nose.

Neither Eliza nor Harry had any idea who he had spoken to. They looked at each other and then around *Diane*.

In unison, the small black shadows elevated, converged, and gracefully hovered.

Four of them took possession of Milton, Justin, Kyle, and Leo while the other took possession of Austin.

*

Elizabeth and Melanie waited until Lisa returned to the kitchen. They tiptoed along the landing and eavesdropped from the top of the stairs.

The entity's wingspan did not intimidate Lisa. 'What did you think you stood to gain by coming here?' She clenched her fists by her sides and scowled. 'And how dare you tell tales on me?' Her chest tightened. 'You're trying to turn my own mother against me by putting ideas in her head.' She paused to catch her breath. 'It's obvious to anyone who can see that you've got a hold over Melanie. Perhaps you've promised her something in return for helping you.' She would not let the entity see her struggle. 'But she's never seen you looking like this before, as she? Her facial expression proved that.' She felt sure that someone else was in the room and turned her head to check. An idea came to mind. She looked up at the entity again. 'You've been manipulating Eliza, haven't you? You've been getting inside her head and making her think she was having bad thoughts. But your scheming went too far when you made her frighten my son. Or was that your intention?'

The black shadow hesitated before it moved from beside the entity and hovered behind her.

'I'm going to ask you nicely to stop stalking me and my son. You need to find someone else to hang around with because you're not wanted here.' She gestured as if she were a teacher who dismissed a naughty pupil from her classroom. 'Get out of this house and never return.'

The entity transformed back into its Damian guise.

'I've got to admit though, that's a pretty cool trick.' She raised an eyebrow.

Unsure as to why she mocked him, he scowled.

'When you change into human form, you're always dressed; how's that even possible?' Her hand motioned, up and down, at his attire. 'You remind me of one of those superheroes or that man who turns green and gets bigger when he's angry.' She smirked. 'Of course, I know you're not one of them, but I'm interested to know if you've ever discovered your undies on the outside of your trousers?' She felt hot despite the clouds of vapour she exhaled.

He looked down to check his attire and felt relieved to see his underwear was not on display.

With a slight frown, she continued through gritted teeth, 'Now get out of here.' Her eyes narrowed. 'If I see you near me or any of my family again, I'll make sure that when I do send you back to Hell, you aren't ever able to return. Do I make myself clear?'

He lowered his head. A moment later he dared to speak as if he had picked up the courage to ask the teacher's permission to go to the toilet, 'Could I tell Mel I am leaving?'

She pointed to the side door. 'It's doubtful Melanie will want to go with you, especially now she's seen you for what you really are. I'm sure she wouldn't feel safe anywhere near you. I think it'd be best for everyone concerned if you left her alone.' She paused. 'I'll tell you what I'll do as a favour to you, not that I owe you anything, after you've left, I'll let her know.'

He looked at his feet as he made his way towards the door. Unaware Elizabeth and Melanie were at the top of the stairs, he stepped outside on to the doorstep. He lifted his head, as though he was a proud man, looked down the drive and saw there was no way he could exit via that route.

Lisa was a few steps behind him. 'You'll have to swim.' She slammed the door shut. As she made her way back towards the kitchen, she sensed Elizabeth and Melanie were watching and presumed they had overheard.

Damian made his way towards the jetty. He looked at Milton, Justin, Austin, Kyle, and Leo who hovered overhead.

Like wide-eyed dangling puppets, they waved their arms about. They were clueless as to what went on and were not in control of their own actions.

Unbeknown to Eliza and Harry, the black shadow had returned and hovered beside Peter.

Peter wondered if the flying men might collide. He put his hand over his mouth to try to stifle his giggle.

Damian glanced across at him and then up at Robert's men, who flew in a circular motion, above his head.

Without warning, in turn, the men swooped like scavenging birds and looped around Damian's head before they rejoined the circle.

Damian kept calm and walked on. He had not noticed the corpse beside the willow and fell on top of it. As he pushed against it, to get to his feet, its stomach wobbled like a plate of jelly.

On his feet again, he looked down at his attire and screwed up his face. He kicked the corpse in the ribs, twice. He wiped his bloodied hands on his clothes and got annoyed when all he did was spread the mess further. He checked around, looked up at the sky, raised his arms above his head and transformed into the winged entity. He ascended through the centre of the circling men and then flew over the lake.

Eliza and Harry ducked and shielded their heads with their arms.

'Wow.' Peter watched the entity until it became a dot in the sky.

In a line, the five men soared over *Diane* and stopped over the middle of the lake. They plunged into its depths where they would never resurface to take another breath.

*

Spencer, who had not seen the activity in the sky, stared at the gate; his mind was blank; his face void of emotion. Whatever had stopped him from pushing the intercom button earlier, made him look at the ground. Blood streamed under the gate. One of the streams neared his feet. He stepped back, turned round to look at his colleague and said, 'We need to get in there, and quick.' He pointed at the blood, made his way towards the intercom and pressed the button. Neither his instincts nor anything else tried to stop him.

There was no response. Was the intercom faulty?

He pressed the button again. It fell off and landed on the ground. The sound from a blown fuse and flying sparks followed. As he stepped back to consider how he might gain entry, he trod in one of the streams and did not notice the blood splashes on the back of his shoe and trouser leg. He looked around the gate, unsure of what he might find; something to give him inspiration. There was no way he could get over the gate without a ladder. He might have tried to climb the wall beside the gate with the overgrowth if he had been twenty years younger, several pounds lighter and did not have an old sports injury on his knee.

He was sure he heard someone, a murmur on the other side of the gate. Was someone there to let him in? He waited for the gate to open or to see if he heard the voice again.

One of the officers, who had only seconds to live, had heard Spencer on the other side. He tried to warn him, but his words dwindled, 'Get … out … of … here.'

Spencer moved closer to the gate. 'What's going on in there?' Silence. 'Try to remain calm. We've radioed-in for back-up. They're on their way. Shouldn't be much longer.' Streams of blood flowed faster towards the lake. He was worried about what he would find on the other side: definite injuries, probable fatalities. He made his way towards the group who were still gathered halfway along the lane. He thanked them for their help and asked them to go home.

The neighbours nodded and made their way to the end of the lane where they chatted briefly before they left. They would read the updates in the local newspaper; a gruesome story, which involved multiple gunshots, was bound to make headline news.

*

Peter and the black shadow had heard the stranger's voice. They looked towards the gate. The small black shadows returned and watched over Peter while the black shadow went to investigate.

*

Lisa looked out of the kitchen window. She glanced across at the corpse beside the willow. 'We need to get rid of the bodies.' She turned round and looked at Elizabeth and Melanie. 'Any suggestions?' She made her way towards the refrigerator and grabbed the last small carton of juice.

Melanie shrugged. She had never disposed of a body before; let alone several. She had presumed they would report what had happened to the police. She looked at Elizabeth for ideas.

Elizabeth watched Lisa jab the straw into the carton and waited until she had slurped every drop. 'We need to ring the police,' she said. 'It's the right thing to do. What else is there?'

'We could bury, burn or dump them in the middle of the lake along with the others.' Lisa, who no longer cared, sounded blasé. All she wanted was to get some rest because she felt ill and exhausted.

Elizabeth's mouth opened in shock. 'One of those bodies happens to be my husband … your stepfather.' She narrowed her eyes. 'What's wrong with you?'

150

'Go on, ring the police.' Lisa picked up Elizabeth's mobile phone from the kitchen table and held it out to her. 'You can tell them what's happened to all those officers they sent here. And when they ask questions about your husband's dodgy dealings, you can explain how you knew nothing about any of it. You can pretend you didn't realise what was happening right under your nose.'

'But I didn't know anything; I swear.' Elizabeth shook her head.

'Really?' *How can anyone not realise what their partner is doing?* Unaware her lips had turned a hint of blue, Lisa continued, 'And if I find it hard to believe you, the police, who, I'm presuming, know nothing about you, will find it a struggle.' She felt light-headed and leant against the sink. 'It's not the first time you've lied either, is it? Or ignored the obvious?' The words were out. She could not take them back.

Elizabeth made her way towards the wine cellar door, opened it, flicked on the light switch and went down the steep stone steps. She slipped half-way, grabbed the handrail, and regained her balance. As she reached the bottom, the hairs on the back of her neck stood on end. *Why's it colder than usual down here?* She gave the temperature no further consideration as she picked a bottle of Chardonnay from one of the racks; well, more of a whichever bottle her hand touched first sort of a moment than a preference.

The ceiling lights flickered and went out simultaneously. She fumbled about in the darkness and made her way back towards the steps. There was no natural light as the cellar door had closed. She fumbled for the handrail, looked up at the filtering light under the door and clambered up the steps. When she reached the top, she searched for the handle, pushed open the door and with her hand still on the handle, she stood in the kitchen.

An illusion appeared behind her. She turned round and was taken back to that fateful day when the door had jammed. Time slowed down. She watched as the closed-door shook. The handle moved up and down several times before the door opened. She felt an odd sensation as the door passed through her. A past representation of herself stood in the doorway before that also passed through her; the odd sensation strengthened. She spun round to see what happened next, but the illusion faded.

She opened and closed the door several times. Not once did it stick. She examined the hinges and the handle; found there was nothing wrong with either and then she closed the door again.

Neither Lisa nor Melanie had moved. They watched Elizabeth with bewilderment. What had she seen? They noticed the bottle in her hand with a thick cobweb dangling from its neck.

Unaware Elizabeth was an alcoholic, Melanie made no judgement. She saw nothing more than a mother who grieved for her child.

Lisa made no comment, but when Elizabeth put the bottle on the worktop, she made it obvious what she thought when she frowned.

It was the illusion and not the look on Lisa's face that made Elizabeth decide not to open the bottle. 'What happened exactly on the day Susan died?' she said to Lisa.

Lisa checked her watch but paid no heed to the time. The foul lingering taste had worsened as if she had sucked on a penny. Her mouth filled with saliva. She had to spit but gulped instead. 'I don't know, Mum, I wasn't here, was I?' Which was not a lie as she was not privy to the exact details.

'I don't think Susan's death was an accident,' Elizabeth said. 'I think she was murdered. In fact, I'm certain she was.' She raised her eyebrows and stared at Lisa; hopeful Lisa would reveal information that might help her to understand what had happened.

'Who by? When the accident happened, there was only you, Peter and Bill nearby.'

Elizabeth was taken aback by her answer. Something did not add up. She looked at her mobile phone and thought about ringing the police. 'Bill who?' she said.

Lisa wanted to kick herself. *What did I have to go and mention him for?* She tried to sidetrack, 'And you still haven't told me what caused that burn on the back of *my* son's neck?'

Elizabeth raised her eyebrows and said, 'I don't know anything about a burn. I never saw how he got it. I presumed it was something to do with the fire.' She paused and recalled their earlier conversation. 'Was Bill the man on that boat? I watched him and Susan flirt like a couple of teenagers. It was shortly after that we discovered her body.' Her eyes welled up. 'I didn't know what his name was. I never got the chance to ask her.' Her eyes widened. 'Hang on, weren't you seeing someone called Bill? I never did get to meet him.' She shook her head. '*Please* don't tell me it was him.'

'I thought you mentioned his name earlier.' Lisa knew her response sounded lame, but questioned why Elizabeth seemed more interested in Bill, a man she had never met, than how a burn had appeared on the back of her grandson's neck.

'No, I couldn't have, like I've already said, I had no idea what his name was.' Elizabeth narrowed her eyes. 'Were you jealous of your sister and him?' She paused to give Lisa a chance to answer. 'I'm right, aren't I?' She nodded.

Lisa was more disappointed than jealous.

'I'm going to ask you one last time.' Elizabeth poised her index finger in front of Lisa's face. 'Did you have anything to do with your sister's death?'

Lisa saw the anger in her eyes. 'Are you serious, Mum? You are aware that he is my son's father, aren't you?' She scowled, shook her head and then looked at the floor. 'I still don't see what any of this as to do with you thinking Susan was murdered. Are you insinuating it was me? Do you think I had something to do with it?'

Their conversation got louder. 'Well, while *my* Susan was being murdered, someone or something made sure I was trapped in the wine cellar.'

'And you think that had something to do with me?' Lisa snorted. 'And why were you in the wine cellar? Were you in there when you said you'd gone back in the house to get Peter another book?'

Melanie listened. Despite what she stood to gain at the end of the day, she still did not like to see a mother and daughter argue. Damian's promise was the reason she had got involved, but would what he had said still stand because he had left? Why had she not realised before what he was, after what he had promised her? She felt alone, out of her depth, and saw no way out.

'What is that black shadow?' Elizabeth sounded calmer. Raised voices were getting them nowhere. 'And the smaller ones beside it?'

I wonder how long she's been able to see them. Why has she not mentioned it before? Lisa did not want to answer. Why was she the only one who answered any questions?

'They follow you around. What are they?'

'What black shadow? I've got no idea what you're talking about.' The corners of Lisa's mouth turned down when she shook her head.

'*Please* tell me what you are?' Elizabeth felt guilty. Was she the reason her daughter was what she was? She had not experienced an easy pregnancy. Her first husband, John, had upset her many times with his acts of violence, and there had been arguments; too many to count. Had those negative feelings passed on to Lisa while she was in the womb?

'I'm your daughter … remember? That little bundle of joy you brought home from the hospital all those years ago.' Her speech sounded slurred. 'I know what you're thinking: you're wishing you'd had me aborted aren't you?' She struggled to keep her eyes open.

The sound of an approaching boat created a welcome distraction.

Lisa looked out of the kitchen window. A police watercraft approached. She could not allow anyone else to step foot on the jetty. There had been enough bloodshed for one day. If she did not try to stop the police, they would see the corpse near the willow and their colleagues crushed against the gate.

There was not enough time to move the corpse from beside the willow or to run upstairs to grab a blanket to cover him. She scanned the kitchen. *Where does Mum keep her tablecloths?* A drawer slid open. She hurried across and rummaged through a pile of white tablecloths. There were no green ones that would camouflage with the lawn. But why would there be? Did anyone own a green tablecloth? She grabbed one from the top of the pile which had an intricate lace trim. It would have to do. She did not have time to be choosy. Maybe if the police looked across, they might believe it was a picnic blanket. She stepped outside with the tablecloth behind her, made her way towards the willow and threw it over the corpse. The feet and the top of the head were still uncovered.

*

With his feet hovering over the pedals, ready to set off at a second's notice, Dobson gripped the steering wheel. As he watched his colleague, he felt the clutch pedal start to lower. He slid his foot sideways, looked at the pedal, and watched as it lowered further.

There was a click sound to the left of him. He turned his head to check where the noise came from. At first, all was still, but then the gearstick slowly moved into the reverse slot and then the handbrake lowered. The van started to move backwards. He felt drowsy and unable to move. Whoever, or whatever, controlled the van must have occupied the same space as him. The notion filled him with dread.

Spencer had heard the van move. He turned to see the look of horror on his colleague's face, and the van as it reversed down the lane. When he chased after the van, it stopped straightaway and waited.

He opened the passenger door and got in. Before he had had chance to fasten his seatbelt, the van started to reverse again. His door, which was ajar, opened and struck every bush and branch that got in the way.

He turned his head and looked at his colleague, who stared out of the windscreen, and said, 'We need to get out of here. You've obviously got the same idea.' He realised he could not hear the engine and looked at his colleague's feet. The pedals moved on their own. He blinked several times and shook his head. Was the van rolling? It was impossible as the lane inclined in the opposite direction. Who controlled the van? Why didn't his colleague try to press the brake pedal? Without warning, the passenger door slammed shut and the van sped up. He grabbed his seatbelt as he fell forward.

Dobson could not grab his seatbelt. His head jerked forward, and his neck cracked.

The van skidded to a halt at the end of the lane.

Wide eyed, Spencer gripped the sides of his seat and revealed the whites of his knuckles. His mouth gaped as he turned to look at his colleague who still gripped the steering wheel. What would happen next? He waited.

Dobson could move again. He turned his head to look at Spencer, checked around and then noted he was still behind the steering wheel. He frowned. *How did we get to the end of the lane?* He turned the key in the ignition. The engine did not start. Every symbol on the dashboard lit up. The gearstick was moved into the first gear slot. The van moved forward. The steering wheel veered to the left. He grappled with it and tried to straighten up, but something stopped him. He pushed against the brake, but his efforts proved futile.

The van approached the lakeside. They had to evacuate, and fast, but as they reached for their unlocked doors, neither would open.

Something flew towards the windscreen. Both officers ducked. Whatever the object was, it struck with a thud. From the chipped windscreen, three cracks continued towards the seal.

The van slowed down. The officers unwrapped their arms from over their heads and turned to look at each other. Was their dilemma over? Anxious as to what they might see, both raised their heads and peeked over the dashboard.

The van was in the lake when the windscreen exploded. It started to fill with water as it continued to edge forward until it was submerged.

*

Peter watched Lisa as she made her way towards the police watercraft. He noticed even though she looked ill, she still tried to act her usual self.

The watercraft pulled up beside Lisa. Officer Ellis switched off the engine. Officer Weatherford threw her the mooring line.

'Hi,' she said as she tied the line to the jetty.

Both officers nodded and got out.

Peter, who still watched over the side, needed to divert their attention before they noticed the carnage. He waved enthusiastically and shouted, 'Hi.'

They looked up at him. Ellis offered a hesitant smile while Weatherford remained pensive.

No one could have failed to notice Peter's enthusiasm as he gestured to the officers to join him.

As though hypnotised, they walked along the jetty and climbed up the ladder.

*

Lewis, another of Robert's men, pointed at the tablecloth on the lawn. 'We need to get across there.' He made his way towards the willow. 'We need to move Charles's body before one of the coppers notice him.'

The others nodded and followed.

Edwin, the shortest of his men, was chosen to keep vigil. Noah, Daryl, Conroy, and Rufus grabbed a limb each. Without a sound, they lifted the corpse and shuffled towards the drive.

With no real interest, Peter glanced across at them.

The bloodstained tablecloth slipped from Charles's corpse and settled on a rose bush. They laid the corpse beside Robert's. Edwin grabbed the tablecloth as he hurried after the others.

Uncertain as to what their next move should be, the men stepped back and looked at the officers pinned against the gate.

*

Elizabeth and Melanie looked out of the kitchen window.

'I'm not even sure why I'm here anymore,' Melanie said. 'I know what Damian told me, but I'm finding it hard to believe your daughter is a demon in disguise and that she's responsible for my daughter's death.' She shook her head. 'Then again, I was fooled by him.' She realised she made matters worse and paused before she continued, 'But even if she is, what can I do? Vicky's not going to be waiting for me when I get home, is she?' She turned her head to look at Elizabeth for an answer or reassurance. 'And all this that's going on around us has got way out of control.'

Elizabeth's thoughts were elsewhere. She had not heard. Damian had divulged some questionable information. It was obvious for anyone to see that he was a demon, but was Lisa also a demon or had he

160

lied? And if Lisa was, why had she not noticed? Had Lisa's guise ever slipped? Why hadn't she paid more attention? And despite the conversation she had overheard between Lisa and him, she was still not convinced. 'I haven't even grieved for my daughter and now I've lost my husband.' She looked across at the bottle of wine. 'I don't know what's going on any more.'

*

Neither Ellis nor Weatherford paid any attention to Harry or Eliza who watched on from behind.

'Hello, young man,' Ellis said. His voice sounded robotic like someone prompted him.

Weatherford's face was void of emotion as he leant forward, put one hand on Peter's shoulder and tousled Peter's hair with the other.

'Grandad's boat,' Peter said excitedly.

'Are you okay?' Weatherford said. His voice sounded robotic too. He did not blink as he looked Peter in the eye.

Peter turned his head and looked at the officer's hand, which still covered his shoulder, and then back up at the officer's face. He frowned. What an odd question: why wouldn't he be, okay?

The officer moved his hand from Peter's shoulder.

Ellis could not see beyond *Diane*'s perimeter as he looked around. He noticed Harry and Eliza.

Harry and Eliza looked away and sat up straight.

The officer noted their apprehension. He was about to question them, but as though distracted, he turned his head to one side. He made his way towards

161

the bow where once again he was able to see beyond *Diane*'s perimeter. He surveyed the jetty and looked up towards the house. His eyes were drawn to the darker patch of grass beside the willow. He squinted, but still could not work out what the darker patch was. Were there any signs of life in the garden? He looked around. There were a few parked vehicles, but he could not see anything untoward.

*

Elizabeth walked towards the French doors, opened them wide, stepped outside and inhaled deeply.

Melanie followed.

'Put on your best smile,' Elizabeth said through gritted teeth.

They made their way towards the jetty.

Elizabeth's exaggerated swagger disguised her anguish. As the officer looked in her direction, she waved. Melanie, however, stared at the back of Elizabeth's head the whole time and tried not to look across at the bloodstained lawn.

Both officers knew something was amiss, but the idea had never crossed their minds to alight and check the property themselves. Instead, they watched as Elizabeth and Melanie boarded.

Elizabeth smiled at Harry and Eliza. She looked around for Lisa. 'Where's Mummy?' she said to Peter.

He shrugged. He had not seen her since she helped moor the police watercraft.

She sat down beside Peter. Melanie sat down to the other side of him.

'Can you tell me what's going on here, Mrs Caplin?' Ellis said.

Elizabeth noticed his lack of enthusiasm. *Why does everyone around here seem to know who I am?* 'I wish I knew, myself.' Which part did he want her to explain? Her entire day had merged into a blur. She had no idea of where to start with her interpretation of events.

Ellis turned to look at the water. He became mesmerised by something no one else could see.

For what felt like an age, no one spoke or moved.

Elizabeth, Harry, Eliza, and Peter watched Ellis as he reached for his truncheon.

Ellis turned round, made his way towards Weatherford and whacked him on the side of his head. His arm was still poised mid-air, about to strike again, when he put his arm down, clambered up on to a bench and on to the edge of *Diane*. He positioned himself, as if he was on a diving board, and lunged forward. He did not land in the water; instead, he crashed, head first, into the watercraft.

Eliza's eyes widened.

Harry moved only his eyes to look at the others.

Elizabeth, who had seen the black shadow enter Ellis's body before he gave that fatal blow, covered her mouth with her hand to stifle any noise.

'Whoops.' Peter giggled.

Horrified by his reaction, Elizabeth decided not to say anything; he was still young and did not know any better. She turned her head to look at Melanie, who was rigid as if rigour mortis had set in.

Melanie, who wanted to go home, stared at the deck. She had cringed when she heard Weatherford's skull split open and Ellis as he crashed into the watercraft.

Still excited at the thought of what might happen next, Peter grinned.

Everyone, except Melanie, stared at Weatherford's severed head, whose eyes were still wide and his mouth still open, and the pool of blood.

No one spoke. No one knew what to say.

*

Lisa, who was seated, cross-legged, beside the bloodstained grass, looked pensive.

Elizabeth looked across at her and decided to join her as she still had a few unanswered questions.

With blurred vision, Lisa watched her approach. Each time she blinked, she kept her eyes closed for a couple of seconds, hopeful of improvement.

Elizabeth sat down beside her. They looked across the lake and tried to ignore the gruesome reality of the corpses that surrounded them.

Elizabeth tried not to look obvious as she examined Lisa's face. *What am I supposed to be looking for? Maybe there's a clue. Something different about the way she looks.* 'Did you see what happened on the boat?' she said.

Lisa nodded. Her blurred vision had returned to normal.

An uncomfortable silence seemed to last longer than real time before Elizabeth dared to pick up the courage and said, 'Who are you?' But was she ready for the answer?

Lisa turned her head to look at her. Her eyes welled up. The corners of her lips turned down.

Of course, she knew what she was, but was that the existence she wanted? She had no life choice. No means of escape. It was the way life would always be. An eternity of rebirths in human form. Never the kind of demon that transformed into a black shadow or a winged entity.

Lisa saw visions of long forgotten memories manifest behind Elizabeth. Former lives, where she had taken on male and female forms, going back centuries.

The recollection became too much for her to watch and made her head spin. She closed her eyes to the peacefulness of darkness.

'What's happening here exactly? Do you know? Can you tell me? I promise I won't get mad. I know you can't help yourself.' Elizabeth was desperate for answers; to the point where she wanted to shake her.

Lisa opened her eyes. The manifestation dispersed. How could she even begin to answer Elizabeth's questions? If only for one lifetime, she longed to be normal and to be accepted. She looked and functioned like any other human, felt love and pain, but she would never be.

A clean-up operation was under way. Robert's men moved the vehicles away from the gate. Elizabeth watched for a while before she turned to

Lisa again, took a deep breath and said, 'How long have you known that you're different?'

The realisation of what Lisa was had only recently become clear. As to an exact time, she could not pinpoint. 'If truth be known, probably most of my life.' She continued to look across the lake.

'And how long have the black shadows been with you?'

Lisa knew the answer, but she shrugged. They had always been with her.

Elizabeth took a deep breath. 'What are we going to do with all these bodies?' She looked around.

Another uncomfortable silence followed before she realised, she would not get any more answers. But as she tried to get to her feet, Lisa grabbed her arm and stopped her. Tears rolled down her cheeks as she turned to Lisa and said, 'We've got ourselves into a right mess here, haven't we? I need you to talk to me. I need to make sense of how we got to this stage.'

'Have you any idea who that is?' Lisa pointed to the black shadow who watched them from *Diane*.

Elizabeth shook her head. She had never given any thought to the black shadow being a someone, let alone someone she might know.

'It's Peter.'

Elizabeth's frown turned into a smile. 'I know that. I thought you meant the black shadow.'

'I do.' Lisa let go of Elizabeth's arm and waited for her to realise.

Elizabeth's eyes widened. 'My Peter?' She put her hand on her chest, over her heart. 'Peter Hurst? Your real father?' Her smile vanished and her eyes revealed regret.

'Yes.' Lisa nodded. A tiredness, like she had never experienced before, overwhelmed her and forced her to rest her eyes.

Elizabeth looked across at the black shadow. 'It can't be.' She shook her head.

'His soul is inside.'

'Inside?' Elizabeth frowned. 'What do you mean, his soul is inside? I don't understand.'

Lisa opened her eyes; the whites had reddened. 'Don't worry. He's safe.' She licked her cracked lips. 'There're other souls in there to keep him company.'

'Are the other souls trapped?' Was Elizabeth oblivious to Lisa's obvious deterioration?

'Well, yes and no. But don't ask me how many because I've no idea. Some were collected before my rebirth.' Lisa's struggle to keep her eyes open continued. She closed them again, as though she had lost her battle, and as quickly as they closed, they opened again. 'It might look like some of the souls are trapped. Depends on your viewpoint. Some of the souls hadn't realised they were looking for an escape route from their mundane lives. Others were bad people. Some of the souls enjoy existing in there.' When she paused to breathe, she heard her chest rattle like a snake. 'I like to think *my* Curator Angelus is doing the world a favour.' She rested her eyes again, for a moment, before she continued, 'Look at it this way, humans are either relinquished of their constant pain or are stopped from inflicting themselves on to others.'

Elizabeth considered Lisa's words: *she believes that shadow is helping humanity. She refers to it like it's a personal possession. But it took my Peter before she was born. Was he a bad person or someone looking for an escape route? I'm sure he was neither. So why did it take the love of my life?* 'Has your Curator Angelus ever taken a good soul?'

Lisa did not answer. The black shadow had captured many innocent souls. It considered it a necessary task and it would continue to take other innocent souls that got in its way. No one or nothing could stop it.

Elizabeth knew the answer from the silence. 'And what about you?'

'What about me?' Lisa, who had grown tired of all the questions, scowled.

'Are you trapped? Do you collect souls?' Elizabeth wanted to understand what she had brought into the world.

'Yes, I suppose you could say I'm trapped.' Lisa tried not to laugh. Her chest tightened. 'Every time I'm reborn, I'm forced to take on human form. I can't come through into this world as a black shadow, or a winged entity, and I can't change shape. That's the kind of *demon* I am, as you put it.' She coughed. It felt like she had been stabbed in the back of her throat. 'And yes, I do help to collect souls. It's our purpose.'

'Why didn't I see any of this before?' Elizabeth said. 'And why me?'

'I've only recently remembered.'

'Honestly?'

'What did you expect? Do you think I grew up knowing what I am? Do you think I look at myself in the mirror every day and see a little red monster with two horns on the top of my head? I admit, I should have realised earlier. I always have done in past lives, but I blame a certain individual from stopping me in this one. That same person inadvertently reminded me to delve deeper and that's when everything clicked into place; although, the realisation did hit me like a shot of adrenaline straight to the brain.' Lisa paused. Had she answered all of Elizabeth's questions? She licked her lips again and made them smart. One of the other questions popped into her head. 'What do you mean, why me?'

'Why was *I* the one who was chosen to give birth to you? What did I do wrong?'

'You sound like you wish you hadn't.' Lisa did not wait for an answer. 'Do you think you're the only one? Do you think I'm the only one? There are thousands of us, tens of thousands. Some haven't realised yet.' She paused to allow Elizabeth time to ponder. 'We come in many forms, and we've got a right to be here just like humans or any other animal. Our existences counterbalance.'

Had Elizabeth understood? Had she wanted to? Had she even heard what had been said? Her attention was drawn towards the men who moved the officers' corpses. 'Do you have any feelings at all?' she said.

169

'Of course, I do. Why wouldn't I? I feel love and both physical and emotional pain. I *do* have a heart you know.'

'But you've killed so many people.' At that moment, Elizabeth realised Lisa could hurt her, if she did anything wrong, but knew she had nothing to fear. She remembered her as a sweet child. Like hurried short film clips, played in chronological order, from innocent child to confident young woman. Forgotten snippets appeared, in and amongst, memories of John's punishments. With every incident, Lisa pleaded for him to stop. An expression of relief on his face as he released his frustration. Had Elizabeth's subconscious blocked out some of the bad memories? She questioned why those memories had chosen to resurface. Had she always watched from the side line and never intervened?

Lisa could see that Elizabeth was deep in thought. She wondered what went through her mind. 'Though not with my own hands,' she said.

A moment later, Elizabeth snapped out of her daydream. She shook her head and said, 'No, that's true, but you get one of your henchmen to do the deed. It's wrong. Don't you see?' She wondered if John might be the reason as to why Lisa had grown up to be evil. Had he knocked the devil into her? Many times, she had heard the saying and had wondered what it meant. Did the definition stare her in the face?

'Only by human rules; not ours.' Pain coursed through Lisa's body and made it harder for her to think of a plausible explanation. 'Look at the situation another way. The human population is too great for the planet to cope with. We provide a solution. We get rid of the ones who want to die or choose to be bad.'

Elizabeth believed Lisa's behaviour was not John's fault. Their parents had punished them in the same way when they had been naughty, and it had not done them any harm. 'But why was I the one who was chosen to give birth to you?'

'You weren't chosen.' Lisa rolled her eyes. 'It happens to unsuspecting expectant mothers every day. I'd say you were one of the lucky ones; privileged even.' She paused. 'I don't think you've grasped what I've told you.'

For a moment, Elizabeth tried to understand what Lisa had said. 'What about Susan? Is she dead because of you?'

Lisa's pupils had dilated. She turned to look at Elizabeth and shrugged. 'I can't be sure.' Which was the truth. She had not intended to appear obstinate. 'I don't know.' Did Elizabeth believe her? 'I can't deny I wasn't angry with Susan and Bill.' Her attention was drawn towards Peter. 'They betrayed me in the worst way imaginable. I was going to let my feelings settle before I asked her about him and then give her a chance to explain.' She paused. 'I saw them kissing, you see. Before I knew what was happening, Bill and I were chatting over coffee. For a while, it felt like old times. He told me she meant nothing to him, and it was her that did all the running, but I still wanted to hear her side of the story.'

'You didn't give the order to have her murdered?'

'Not that I'm aware of, but it's not as simple as that. I don't always give *the order*. Sometimes it just happens.'

The conversation had been too deep for Elizabeth to follow, hence her frown. All she wanted was a straight answer, a simple yes or no. But she felt she would not hear either of those words any time soon. *Maybe she's not behind Susan's murder; after all, who would kill their own sister? But if she wasn't, who was?*

*

Eliza watched Peter who studied Weatherford with an unhealthy interest.

Peter jumped off the bench and made his way towards the corpse. He crouched beside it, reached forward, and moved its head to enable him to get a better look at the wound, which was several inches long and had split open as if his scalp had been unzipped. He poked his index finger inside, so he could get a glimpse of the skull. His foot slid sideways. When he looked at the deck to investigate, to his horror, he saw he was standing in a puddle of blood. Straightaway, he straightened up and wiped his shoe on the corpse's trousers before he stepped aside.

She was unsure if she should intervene and move him away. Harry had the same thought, but neither of them did anything. Melanie continued to stare at the deck.

Peter walked around to the other side of the corpse. He checked for blood before he knelt and leant over it. He pressed his fingers to the side of its neck. A few seconds later, he jumped up and said, 'He's dead.'

Harry and Eliza turned to look at each other. Neither of them needed to say anything as they knew what the other thought.

Peter clambered on to the bench and looked over the side at Ellis. 'And he's dead too,' he said.

Chapter Twelve

The Clean-up

There had been no further gunfire or skirmishes. The only sound was from distant birds as the night sky drew in.

'Do you think it's safe for us to go and join Lisa and Mrs Caplin?' Eliza said to Harry and Melanie.

Up until that moment, he had been undecided if he should go home or stay and offer his support. He nodded in response. He believed Mrs Caplin was a kind woman and she did not deserve any of what happened to her.

Melanie continued to stare at the deck in front of her feet.

*

Still seated on the lawn, neither Lisa nor Elizabeth had spoken for a while. Moisture had soaked through to their skin. Had they not noticed? Lisa tried to stay awake, but every time she dozed, her head flopped forward and made her sit up with a start. Elizabeth divided her attention between Lisa and Peter, who looked over the side of *Diane* into the watercraft as if he expected Ellis's corpse to change into a zombie.

*

Apprehensive about what might happen next, Harry and Eliza got to their feet and made their way along the deck. In unison, they turned their heads to check on Peter and Melanie, looked up at the sky and then alighted.

As they made their way along the jetty, the small black shadows moved aside. Neither of them had seen the shadows, but the hairs on the backs of their necks stood on end. Aware the other had also felt a presence, they glanced at each other, but neither said a word.

Bleary-eyed, Lisa watched as Harry and Eliza approached. A random thought popped into her head: the cooking ingredients for their dinner were still in the back of Susan's wrecked car. She was not hungry but wondered when Peter had last eaten. She struggled to think; her mind was foggy like something blocked her thoughts. With neither the inclination nor the energy to prop herself up against the stove, she would order them a takeaway later. But how would she explain the carnage to the delivery driver? No, she would have to grab a packet of crisps or a snack from the refrigerator for him.

The clean-up continued. Robert's men collected sheets and covers from the house, wrapped them around the deceased and piled them in the back of one of the vans.

Elizabeth watched as Lewis and Noah placed Robert down beside the rose bushes. *I wonder what they'll do with the bodies.* She had had time to think about the situation her husband had got her into. Her distress had turned to anger. She no longer cared what happened to his body. He had kept secrets from her and no doubt more would be unearthed. The lies had not only affected her but had also put her family in danger. Had he ever given her a second thought?

What would she do once everything had settled? The wedding photograph of Robert's late wife and him, which took pride of place on her mantelpiece, would be the first item to go. She would smash the glass into thousands of pieces and place a match flame to his face.

Eliza sat down beside Elizabeth. Harry, who remained on his feet, close by, was concerned if he sat down, he might struggle to get up again as he had started to get twinges in his lower back.

'Should we help?' Eliza gestured towards the clean-up.

'No.' Elizabeth shook her head. 'Not our mess.' She was convinced the decisions she had made were the right ones. She would no longer allow anyone to tell her what she could or could not do.

'Are you okay? You've had one hell of a day,' Harry said to Elizabeth. 'Would you like me to make you a tea or a coffee?'

'I'm fine, thank you.' She did not look at him.

An uncomfortable silence followed.

Robert's men rushed across the lawn to collect Weatherford's and Ellis's bodies.

As the officers' bodies were removed from *Diane* and the watercraft, Melanie still did not raise her head to look at what went on; however, Peter's attention alternated as he watched the two activities. His disappointment at the removal of the bodies soon changed to excitement; perhaps he had something else planned.

'How will they get rid of the police boat and all these other vehicles?' Eliza said. 'And I'm sure they'll notice at the station that their men are missing.'

'I'm sure they know what they're doing,' Elizabeth said. 'No doubt, they've had to do something similar before or had a practice run.'

*

Melanie's thoughts had gone back to happier times that she had shared with her late husband George. She wished he were there; he would know what to do. She had pictured Victoria's first smile, giggle, step, and garbled word.

She saw Peter when she lifted her head. He looked across at her. She glanced around *Diane* and was surprised to see they were alone.

'Hi.' She waved. She remembered when Victoria was the same age: a vulnerable little girl in constant need of her mother's love; unlike the little boy in front of her.

'Hi.' His attention reverted to the bloodied deck; fascinated, like a child who waited for an ice-cream and gawked at the ice-lolly choices on the van's window.

Unaware they had company in the form of a black shadow, she said, 'Shall we go and join your mum and your grandma?'

He jumped off the bench and landed on his feet with a thud. *Diane* swayed. The pool of blood rippled. He ran towards her and held out his hand for her to hold.

She hesitated as she felt unnerved by the way he looked at her. Still troubled, she reached for his hand and noticed how warm and small it was.

The black shadow remained still.

Victoria's young face overshadowed Peter's. Melanie imagined his hand was Victoria's too. She helped him alight. They made their way along the jetty.

The small black shadows hovered to the sides.

*

Daryl untied the mooring line, threw it into the watercraft and jumped aboard. With his feet to either side of the pool of blood and other bodily fluids, he looked down and tried to steady himself. With a gloved hand, he leant forward and tried to swish the pool away to allow him to inspect the damage. There was a crack where Ellis's head had made impact; water seeped in. He took off his shoes, wrapped his jacket around them and threw them on to the jetty. He noticed the eery silence and the blanket of thin mist over the water as he checked around the lake. He switched on the engine and made his way towards the middle where he would sink the watercraft and then swim back.

Conroy and Rufus manoeuvred the vans away from the double-doored outhouse, swung the doors open and drove the police vehicles inside. These would be picked up later and taken to the crusher. The firearms would be sold on to the usual dealer.

Dead bodies were easy to dispose of when you knew people in the right professions. An acquaintance of Robert's, who worked at a nearby crematorium, could dispose of them, along with their belongings, in exchange for a favour per person. For his own amusement, the technician would add the ashes to other urns, bit by bit. Unaware, loved ones would later collect the urns.

Another acquaintance, a property developer, could have the bodies covered with concrete in the foundations at one of his building sites for a fee.

However, the disposal of Robert's body was a different issue. He would not be sent to a crematorium or spend an eternity in a concrete grave beneath someone's home. His death needed to be recorded to allow Elizabeth to make a claim on his life insurance.

During the next couple of hours, several visitors called round to the house. Edwin, who was the designated gatekeeper, made the decision if to allow their access. There was no need for Elizabeth's involvement.

Another acquaintance, a Neurosurgeon, arrived on foot with her medical bag. She was there to remove the bullets from Robert. She did not charge a fee; however, she was supplied with cocaine for personal use every first Sunday of the month in return for her immediate services with no questions asked. The procedure was performed in one of the smaller outhouses. Lewis and Noah had lifted him on to a plastic sheet that covered a long wooden work bench. A dimly lit bulb dangled just above the surgeon's head. She had worked under much worse conditions.

Although the procedure was routine, she still worked carefully. She always found her work easier when the patient no longer breathed, and she did not need an anaesthetist, on hand, to help.

She put the extracted bullets into a plastic bag. Her gloved hands were covered with bits of bloodied flesh. She wrapped several layers of toilet paper around the scalpel's blade and put it into the same bag with her disposable gloves and smock. The bag was put in her medical bag before she left without saying a word.

Lewis and Noah re-entered the outhouse to move him. They propped him on a chair, in front of a desk, and leant him against a wall in the far corner.

A van arrived with two men seated in the front. They looked like cage fighters with their shaven heads, bulging muscles, protruding veins, and an abundance of tattoos. Large black letters on the side of their van revealed they were there to carry out a jet washing service. They got out and dressed into waterproof attire. Edwin explained where their services were needed. The two men set to work; again, with no questions asked. They scrubbed away morsels of brain, blood, and any other evidence that had been left behind.

The frogmen would conduct an extensive search of the lake sometime in the future. The watercraft and many bodies would be discovered underneath the silt. It was unlikely anyone would dare to confess they had seen the watercraft moored to the Caplin's jetty.

The police vehicles and Susan's car were collected. They were hidden underneath tarpaulin on the back of recovery trucks on the way to the crusher.

The last of Robert's men and acquaintances left. They drove slowly to minimalize any excessive noise or unwanted attention.

At the rear, Conroy slowed down. Despite the darkness, he still saw the tread marks, which veered off towards the lake, and the flattened bushes where the police van had ploughed through. Was he the only one who had noticed? He tried to remember what the bushes had looked like before. He shook his head and drove on, past the two officers who were inside the van at the bottom of the lake.

The outbuilding with Robert inside was alight. A discarded cigarette had been placed on a pile of papers on his desk. Everyone, who was left behind, had agreed the fire service were not to be called until the building was almost burnt to the ground. More police were expected to call round; after all, many officers were missing. But everyone left behind would plead their ignorance.

*

The chaos had stopped, and peace resumed.

The evening air had cooled. No longer in the garden, Lisa, Peter, Harry, and Melanie were seated around the kitchen table with empty bowls in front of them. Elizabeth warmed a large pan of tomato soup on the hob. Eliza buttered sliced white bread and waited for the kettle to boil.

Harry thought it strange how he would not see Mr Caplin around the place any more. He got to his feet, strolled towards the window, and rubbed his hands together. He tried to look out into the garden but could not see beyond his reflection.

Eliza put a plate of bread in the centre of the table. Hopeful she had remembered what everyone had asked for with requests of tea, coffee, no sugar, no milk, or not too strong, she dashed back towards the kettle.

Peter struggled to stay awake. He rested his forehead on the tabletop. Lisa got to her feet and pulled out his chair. She gave him time to raise his head before she lifted him and rested him against her shoulder. Her arms were weak, and he felt heavier than usual like he had had three big meals with plenty of snacks in-between. He closed his eyes as she carried him through the living room and up the stairs. She reached the top and dragged her feet along the landing towards their bedroom. As she laid him down, she took one look at his pillow and for a moment was tempted to lay down beside him.

The kitchen was quiet when she returned. Her mobile phone vibrated in her pocket. The others stopped eating, lifted their heads, and turned to look at her.

She had not expected anyone to call. She reached into her pocket and checked the phone number on the screen. It was not one she recognised. She accepted the call. 'Hello?'

A man's voice greeted her, 'Good evening, Ms Brook. I hope I haven't rung you at an inconvenient time. Are you able to talk?'

The others continued to watch her.

'Wait a minute.' She made her way towards the side door, opened it, and stepped outside. The air was smoke filled. She closed the door behind her and whispered, 'Who is this?'

'It's Beechwood Estate Agency,' he whispered.

'Oh, hi. I'm sorry, I didn't recognise your voice.'

'You asked us to get in touch if a certain property came into our grasp. Well, I have good news, we've had instructions to put your family's old home on the market.'

'Excellent.' A warmth paralleled her aches. She loved it when a plan came together.

'We only got word this afternoon. We haven't started to market the property yet. I thought I'd let you know first.' He paused because he expected her to speak, but when she didn't, he said, 'Are you still interested in the property, Ms Brook?'

'I am, yes.' She held her mobile phone at arm's length and coughed. Her chest rattled. Bloodied spittle flew from her mouth and landed on the doorstep. Her temples pulsated.

'Ms Brook ... are you okay?' *Is she alone? She sounds like she needs medical help. Should I ring for an ambulance?*

She took a deep breath and put the mobile phone against her ear.

He waited a moment before he spoke again, 'Are you okay, Ms Brook?'

'Yes, I'll be okay.'

'If, you're sure.' An uncomfortable silence followed before he picked up the courage and said, 'I feel awful for asking you, but would you like to make an appointment to view the property? I can arrange the appointment with you now, if you like, or I can call back later, if it's not convenient.'

'That won't be necessary.' She took a tissue from her pocket, wiped it across her lips and examined the bloodied smear. 'Thank you, but I already know what the house looks like. I'm a cash buyer. Whatever the asking price is, I'll pay it.' She felt ten times worse than when she had a bad bout of flu a few years earlier. Did she have some sort of virus? She had felt all right when she got up that morning. What had made her deteriorate so quickly? She was sure she would feel better after a good night's sleep.

'Excellent, Ms Brook. I'll pass the necessary paperwork on to your solicitor. If I remember correctly, you left their details when you called in.' He searched his desk. 'Found it.'

'Thank you for calling to let me know. We'll speak soon.' She hung up, crouched in front of the doorstep, and examined the blood speckles. *What's wrong with me?*

She opened the side door and although her health worries clouded her good news, she feigned a smile as she entered. The timing was not right for her to tell Elizabeth about her intended house move; however, she would tell Peter when the two of them were next alone. She made her way towards the kitchen.

'Who was that on the phone?' Elizabeth said.

'Just an old friend.' Lisa looked at the floor.

Why's she lying. What's she hiding? Elizabeth did not pry. She turned to look at Melanie. 'Would you like to stay here tonight? You're more than welcome. There's plenty of room.'

'Thank you, that's very kind.' It was too late in the day for Melanie to make tracks back to Beechwood. *Oh no, I didn't bring a change of underwear or any toiletries with me.*

As if Elizabeth had read Melanie's mind, she said, 'And don't worry about not having a change of knickers or any nightwear with you, I've got plenty of spares still in their wrappers. I'll show you where they are later. You can choose what you want, and you'll find a spare toothbrush in the bathroom cabinet as well.'

'Thank you.'

'It's the least I can do.' She looked at Harry and Eliza. 'The invitation goes out to you two, as well.' Her face reddened. 'Harry, I mean the offer of a spare bed, *not* my underwear.'

Robert's men had neglected to call a glazier to the upstairs broken window and smoke had started to drift inside the house.

Lisa looked out of the kitchen window. She could no longer see where the shadows were.

Mesmerised by the flames, the shadows hovered over the lawn while smoke drifted through them.

She stood on her tiptoes, leant forward and tried to look across at the flames. 'Have we got any wood to board the upstairs window with, Harry?' She was unsure how much longer they should leave it before they rang the fire service. Wouldn't it look suspicious if the fire was left to rage much longer?

'Any suitable wood will be in the outbuilding, next to the one that's on fire. It'll be too dangerous to go and look.'

'Should we call the emergency services?' Eliza said. She knew the plan, along with everyone else, but was worried the flying embers might ignite the surrounding buildings. 'The fire might get out of control.'

'Yes, I think you're right,' Elizabeth said, but she did not reach for her mobile phone or get up to use the landline. Instead, she stared at the floor. Had the realisation of what had happened just dawned on her?

Harry was about to make his way towards the landline when Lisa touched his forearm and stopped him. 'I'll make the call,' she said. She plodded through into the living room, picked up the handset and dialled the emergency services.

Smoke drifted down the stairs.

With a blank expression, Eliza stared out of the French doors. She decided to open them.

The others watched on. No one intervened.

Lisa put down the handset. 'The fire service is already on the way. Someone else rang them. Whoever made the call saw the flames from the other side of the lake.' She turned to look at the others and saw Eliza in the doorway. 'Come in and close the doors.'

Eliza had heard, but she still stepped outside and closed the doors behind her.

Melanie followed.

Eliza made her way towards the fire.

The smoke continued to thicken. The heat intensified. Melanie cupped her hand over her nose and mouth. The air was impossible to breathe. She coughed. What was Eliza's intention? It looked like she might walk into the flames. Why would she do that? Melanie had to stop her. She quickened her pace. When she was within reaching distance, she grabbed Eliza's shoulder.

Eliza spun round. Dazed, as if she had been disturbed while sleepwalking, she rubbed her eyes and looked around, but she was standing in the thick of the smoke. Embers flew around their heads like confused fireflies. Unbeknown to her, she was only several feet from the burning outbuilding. She coughed too. Convinced her eyes might melt, she tried to shield them with her arm and felt every hair singe.

'We need to get back in the house,' Melanie tried to shout above the roaring flames as she pulled Eliza back.

'Yes, yes … of course.' With her arms out in front of her, Eliza made her way back towards the French doors. She stopped a couple of times: once when her coughing became uncontrollable and the other to pick herself up after she had fallen over a bush.

Lisa looked out of the kitchen window to try to see what was going on. Elizabeth and Harry had their faces pressed against the French doors.

When Eliza appeared on the other side of the glass, he opened the door, grabbed her by the arm, and pulled her inside. In the brief time she had been outside, she had blackened and looked like a chimney sweep. He closed the door.

*

Melanie was about to make her way back up towards the house when something forced her to pull back. She turned round and looked towards the flames. Her eyes smarted and the poor visibility made it almost impossible. What was she meant to be looking at?

She struggled to keep her eyes open and tried to fan the smoke away with her hands. Was that an apparition drifting through the flames towards her? It stopped, on the fire's perimeter, where the outhouse doorway used to be.

She focused on Victoria's face. Neither the heat nor her struggle for breath deterred her.

Victoria, whose hair was tied up with a pink scrunchie, was not ablaze. Neither the smoke nor the heat affected her as she held out her arms; an invitation for her mother to join her.

Hesitant, Melanie remembered the day she found a pink scrunchie on the bathroom floor and how her daughter had appeared and then vanished again when she tried to get close to her. What if the same happened again?

Victoria waited.

Although Melanie knew she might be mistaken, and Victoria might be a figment of her imagination, she walked into the flames.

*

'Where's Melanie?' Elizabeth said.

Eliza coughed. 'I thought she was behind me.'

'Maybe she's fallen.' Harry looked out of the French doors. 'I'm sure she'll be here any second.'

The smoke alarm's piercing sound made them all jump. The patter of small footsteps along the landing followed. Peter walked down the stairs. His hand slid down the handrail while his other hand, which was tightened into a fist, rubbed his eyes.

A fire engine's siren drew closer. Flashing lights edged along the lane. The engine stopped on the other side of the gate. Elizabeth was hesitant to let them in; fearful the truth would be revealed, but she knew she had no choice.

The engine pulled into the drive and stopped at the bottom. Its doors opened. Four firefighters jumped out, dressed to tackle the blaze, equipped with breathing apparatus.

One of the firefighters looked up at the house. He thought he saw someone on the other side of the French doors. It was difficult to be sure through the smoke. He made his way up to check. As he looked towards the lake he saw *Diane*, but not the rose bushes that he trampled underfoot.

Harry opened the door. The others joined him.

The fireman lifted his breathing apparatus from his face. 'You need to get out of the house right away.

It's too risky for you to leave by car.' He pointed towards *Diane*. 'Use that.' He counted how many people were there. Four. 'Is there anyone else on the premises who's not here with you?' Peter poked his head out between Lisa and Elizabeth's legs. The fireman smiled. Five.

Elizabeth, who had not wanted to give the game away, kept quiet. Did her frown and lip biting reveal her guilt? Was he already suspicious as to the delay in calling them? She looked at Lisa and waited for her to answer.

'One of our friends: Melanie. She went out a few minutes ago and hasn't returned,' Lisa said.

'Might she have gone near the fire?' He looked up at the broken window. He was not there to make judgements. His concerns were to extinguish fires and save lives.

What plausible reason could there have been for Melanie to go near the fire? They looked at each other, frowned, and shrugged.

'Okay, we'll check. Is there anyone else who isn't accounted for?' the fireman said.

'Not that we're aware of.' Lisa shook her head and tried not to gulp.

The fireman did a double take of her and then looked away.

'My husband, Robert, is away on business,' Elizabeth said. She was surprised by how the words flowed with ease. 'Everyone, except Melanie, is accounted for.' She never faltered as she knew once his remains were found, the plan must be adhered to

190

– no one had realised the outbuilding was on fire until the smell of smoke had drifted in, and the smoke detector alarm had gone off. When they checked through the window, they noticed the hazy orange aura. They had not noticed his car. He must have returned. No one had known. They had no idea why he was in the outbuilding, and yes, he did enjoy the occasional cigarette.

The fireman put his breathing apparatus back on. His voice sounded muffled as he shouted, 'Time to go.' He gestured for them to make their way towards *Diane*, turned round and rushed back towards the fire.

The rest of the fire crew tried to dampen the flames. Water against fire; two of nature's elements in an ultimate showdown.

'Peter, grab your shoes and jacket. We're going on an adventure on Robert's boat,' Lisa said.

He stared at her. He knew she was unwell and that something awful might happen.

'Shoes and jacket. I won't tell you again.'

He did as he was told with no questions asked.

The others had heard her instruction and grabbed their jackets.

Elizabeth picked up *Diane*'s key from the kitchen worktop. It had a silver keyring with the letter *D* engraved on one side of the dog tag. She hesitated a moment. Was the key there earlier? Why wasn't it in the lockbox? No one had sailed on *Diane* for days. Who had put the key on the worktop for her to find? And why had she gone straight to the key without checking the lockbox first?

She left the French doors open and followed the others who made their way towards *Diane*. They tried to shield their faces and intermittently glanced across at the fire.

Halfway, Elizabeth stopped and tried to look around for Melanie. *Where is she?*

'Come on, Mum, keep up,' Lisa shouted. She had also considered Melanie's whereabouts. Could she have gone into the burning outbuilding? But why would she have done that?

Tired and apprehensive, they all boarded *Diane*.

'Where will we go?' Elizabeth said to Harry as she handed him the key.

He was the only one aboard who knew how to sail *Diane* as he had taken it around the lake many times while Mr Caplin entertained guests. He pointed to the other side of the lake. 'We'll wait there until the fire service have put out the fire. I'm sure Mr Smyth won't mind us mooring to his jetty.'

She looked at Lisa and Peter, who both looked subdued. 'But we could be hours,' she said. *Have I made the right decision? Well, it's too late to turn back now.*

'There's nothing I can do, Mrs Caplin. It's a waiting game now.' He turned round and put the key in the ignition.

No one spoke as *Diane* meandered past empty anchored boats, through patches of mist and pockets of ice-cold air. Some looked like they had been there for decades: derelict and rotting.

Mr and Mrs Smyth were happy for *Diane* to be moored to their jetty. After much deliberation, they were the ones who had called the emergency services.

Eliza made up a makeshift bed for Peter on one of the benches, which included a rolled-up jacket for a pillow and a well-used itchy wool blanket; however, it was doubtful any of them would get any sleep.

'You're more than welcome to come and stay with us inside the house,' Mrs Smyth said.

'No, thank you,' Lisa said, hastily, on everyone's behalf.

Mrs Smyth smiled, nodded, and shuffled back up towards the house.

When she was sure she would not be overheard by Mrs Smyth, Elizabeth said, 'What about Peter? Don't you think he'd be more comfortable indoors? He'll be warmer and at least *he'll* get a good night's sleep.'

Peter's eyes widened. He wondered what had happened between his mother and his grandmother.

'He's fine where he is.' Lisa looked across the lake at the soaring flames. *I wonder if there'll be any part of Robert left to identify. He'll have no fingerprints. Will they need to examine his dental records or his DNA profile?*

Mrs Smyth returned with a tray of refreshments: flasks of coffee and tea, and a small jug of orange cordial for Peter. She put the tray down on the jetty. She left and returned with another tray: cups, teaspoons, sugar, and milk. She put that tray on the jetty, beside the other one, smiled up at them on *Diane*, nodded and then shuffled back up towards the house again.

Lisa's mind wandered. She imagined Elizabeth as she made her way through an unkempt graveyard towards a central burial vault. At the bottom of several uneven stone steps, a thick web concealed the entrance. Elizabeth went down the steps, swept her hand through the web, opened the creaking door and entered. Daylight filled the darkened room. She made her way towards an open coffin in the middle of the vault. Bony fingers appeared over the side of the coffin. A skeletal Robert sat upright, turned its head to look at her and grinned.

An explosion on the other side of the lake brought her back to reality.

'What the ...' Harry said.

Everyone ducked.

A little while later, Harry picked up the courage to look over the side. The others kept low and watched him. His attention was drawn towards a plume of billowing black smoke. *I don't think there's any explosives or flammable liquids in any of the outbuildings. I wonder if it was Mr Caplin's car or the fire engine that blew up. I hope none of the firefighters were injured.*

The wind changed direction. Visibility over the lawn became clearer.

Lisa straightened up and stood beside him. 'Any ideas what could have caused the explosion?' She grabbed a pair of binoculars from a hook beside her, adjusted the focus and looked across the lake. Why were the black shadow and the small black shadows still there?

'I'm not sure, but if I had to hazard a guess, I'd say it was Mr Caplin's car that exploded.' He scratched his head as though not convinced.

The binoculars dangled by their strap, around her neck, as she turned to look at him. 'Damn, why didn't anyone think to move his car?'

He sighed. 'I'm worried the explosion might have killed those firemen.' He checked on the situation again. 'And the fire's spread ... look.' He pointed at the Caplins' house.

'Quick, call the emergency services,' Elizabeth shouted up at the Smyth's house. She started to cry. Why had she not called the fire service sooner?

Mrs Smyth ran towards them. Her arms flapped beside her. 'Howard's already rung them. The fire service is already on the way; the fire crew called for backup a while ago.' She stopped on the jetty, put her hands on her hips and took a deep breath. 'When I told the lady, who answered my call, about the explosion, she sounded concerned, but seemed much calmer than what I'm feeling right now.' She tried to smile, but her eyes welled up.

Lisa looked through the binoculars again. *How's the second fire engine going to get in though? It looks like the gate's closed.* Something twinkled over the Caplin's lawn. Was it an orb? More started to appear. Some appeared out of thin air while others drifted in from different directions. She looked across to the right and checked on the firefighters but could not see them. She scanned the garden again. Some of the orbs had transformed into apparitions of their past lives. 'Mum, can you watch Peter for me? I need to get back across there to see what's happening. I've got a niggling feeling Melanie's still there. If she is, she'll need our help. We can't leave her there.' It was a lie, but the right believable excuse she needed.

'That's not a good idea. You need to stay with us,' Elizabeth said.

But Lisa ignored her and got into the life raft. Eliza helped her.

Chapter Thirteen

Infinitus

Spirits had gathered on the lawn of the Caplin residence.

Lisa had no idea what she intended to do when she reached them. She dipped the oars through the mist into the water and started to row. In her weakened state, she struggled. The water felt like thick treacle. A cloud of vapour appeared in front of her face every time she exhaled. She wished she had put on an extra layer of clothes. She wiggled her toes to relieve their numbness and blew warm breath over her hands. A thought came from nowhere: *Mum could see the black shadows.* Her eyes widened. *She's one of us. Does she know?*

The others stayed on *Diane.* Although Harry intended to go nowhere, he still gripped the steering wheel like the ship's captain. Elizabeth and Peter frowned as they looked across at Lisa in the raft. Did Eliza's smirk imply she knew something the others did not?

The roaring flames grew louder as Lisa drew closer.

The spirits, some of whom she recognised, had congregated beside the willow. None of them were troubled by the fire. They watched her with a keen interest. While some of them appeared sympathetic, others were still angered by their untimely demises.

Without warning, the wind changed direction again. Smoke blew across the garden. Security lights came on and emphasised the outlines of the swirling smoke.

It felt like an age before the wind changed direction again. More spirits had appeared. Melanie was one of them. She hovered alone.

What's going on? A throbbing pain ran through Lisa's head. *Why have all these souls been released?* She dropped the oars and massaged her head. A sharp stomach pain made her double over. She felt nauseous, put her hand over her mouth, coughed and aggravated her headache. As she moved her hand from her mouth, she knew what would be on her palm. She rinsed away the blood in the lake. At that moment, she became aware of her own impending death: her palpitations, heightened sense of smell, vibrant yet blurred colours, the sound of her own raspy breathing and memories of past lives. Death was only a matter of time. She closed her eyes and tried to relax. She shivered, yet streams of sweat followed as did the vomit and the diarrhoea. She opened her eyes again; their rawness gave the impression she had cried for hours.

Eliza, who was alone on *Diane*, smiled as she watched Lisa. The others had gone into Mr and Mrs Smyth's house where there was warmth, food and somewhere comfortable to rest their weary heads. Eliza had told them she would follow on shortly as there was something she needed to do.

Lisa looked across at *Diane*. She knew someone was on board, watching her, but could not see who was there.

The winged entity returned and landed behind Eliza. She had expected his return and did not resist as he wrapped a wing around her. She stayed silent as they ascended; awestruck by the night sky.

A defeated, faeces-soaked, Lisa laid down and stared up at the stars. Vomit trickled from the corners of her mouth. *Have those stars always twinkled that bright?* She almost choked as she spluttered blood. *What have Eliza and Damian done to me?*

She had no idea how much time had passed when she heard the winged entity flapping overhead. He landed at her feet. The raft swayed. He transformed into Damian, brushed down his attire with the back of his hand and looked down at her. His lip curled up at one side as he smiled.

I wonder what he's done with Eliza. She imagined taking his legs from under him, with one sweep of her foot, and then he toppled, headfirst, into the water; however, she was too weak to carry out such an action.

'Not so big and tough now, are we?' His image alternated between the winged entity and Damian. Were his abilities weakening or was it a hallucination? 'Where are your family and guardian angel when you need them the most?'

Her mouth opened, but the words inside her head sounded too jumbled to make a coherent sentence, so she remained quiet.

'The thought must have crossed your mind as to why you feel ill and are on the brink of death.' He tapped his index finger on his chin. 'I will give you a clue.' He leant forward and pulled a face as though repulsed by her smell. 'The ones we believe we are the closest to, are usually the reason behind our downfall. They are not always what they seem.'

What's he insinuating? She turned her head to one side. There were only two people in the entire world she loved and trusted. Would Elizabeth or Peter intentionally harm her? They were the only two people she would not have the black shadow take revenge on. She closed her eyes and tried not to cry. *He's lying. Trying to taunt me. I know it's him or Eliza or both who've poisoned me.*

Her breathing slowed. She was sure she felt every drop of blood pass through her veins and its warm flow as it leaked from every orifice. She looked up at him, but it was difficult to see through bloodied eyes. She found the energy to point up at the sky.

Within seconds, his smugness had disappeared. With the stars eclipsed, he knew the two of them were no longer alone.

The black shadow loomed overhead. Although it had disobeyed her instructions to put Peter's life before her own, it had not left him without a guardian as the small black shadows watched over him. A final decision was yet to be made on which of the small black shadows would become his Curator Angelus.

Damian did not need to turn round. He knew what awaited him. He transformed into the entity and stretched out his wings as if he believed himself to be a peacock with beautiful plumage.

The black shadow continued to hover and thwarted any escape attempt by the winged entity; however, the standoff was over in an instant as the black shadow lowered until the two of them occupied the same space.

The winged entity could not delay his destiny. He squealed, like a piglet, as he tried to flap his wings. He surrendered; aware any resistance was futile.

The black shadow had taken control of the winged entity; however, it did not take flight straightaway and looked down at the raft. How much longer would the demon, who was once named Lisa, have to endure living inside an irreparable human shell? It would return to guide the soul.

The black shadow and the winged entity's journey to Hell began.

Darkness prevailed. Lisa closed her eyes and allowed poignant memories to fill her mind.

Roaring flames and stifled laughter interrupted her moment of reflection. Curious as to where the laughter came from, she opened her eyes. She was greeted with familiar darkness; however, she felt free of pain, her nausea had subsided, and her breathing had returned to normal. She sat up and turned her head to look towards *Diane*.

Eliza's face appeared in the distance. Her face drew closer and stopped several inches in front of Lisa's. Her laughter had stopped; however, her smile remained. She said, 'It was neither Damian nor I who poisoned you.' Her face vanished. Darkness resumed.

There was a distant sound of a weeping child. Lisa knew who those tears belonged to. She searched through the darkness and found Peter seated, alone, on a hardwood floor. His shoulders trembled as he pressed his face against his knees and hugged his legs. Was he inside Mr & Mrs Smyth's house? Why was he crying? Why did no one console him?

As she reached out to touch him, his image and the sound of his crying faded.

The fire's roar and the smell of smoke no longer filled the air. She turned her head and tried to focus through the darkness, but there were no flames. Was she looking in the right direction or had the fire been extinguished?

She stayed still and listened for a sound; anything that might give her a clue as to what had happened.

A twinkle in the sky caught her attention. She had returned to the real world. Like an explosion of bullet holes, more stars appeared. The moon's reflection shone on the water. Her mother's home was a burnt-out shell. Where was *Diane*?

The black shadow returned after night had turned to day. It was there to protect and escort the demon who had once lived in Lisa's shell.

It descended and she ascended to join it. She expected to see herself as she looked down, but neither her body nor the raft were there.

When would the demon be reborn? Straightaway or after fifty years? The demon would know when the time was right.

Chapter Fourteen

The Culprit

The morning before Susan's funeral, Elizabeth had taken delivery of some grocery shopping. A pack of small orange juice cartons, the sort with bits in, were in that delivery. She hid them in the bottom of her wardrobe. Lisa was the only one who drank that type of juice; Peter said he thought the bits were nasty.

The idea had not come to her in a dream, but had burst into her head, like a volcanic eruption, when she found several syringes in the bottom of Robert's sock drawer as she tidied away a pile of his clothes. She had no idea why the syringes were in there, but she took one, hopeful it would not be missed, and put it in her dressing gown pocket that hung behind the door.

On the morning of the funeral, she got up early after another restless night. It was still dark outside. Careful not to wake Robert, she pulled back the duvet and got out of bed. She grabbed her dressing gown, wrapped it around her and checked in the pocket; the syringe was still in there. She collected the cartons from the wardrobe and made her way downstairs to the kitchen.

No one else was up. She turned on the spotlights over the sink. After she had checked she was alone, she found a bottle of cleaning agent in the sink cupboard. She unscrewed the lid and put the bottle and the syringe on the drainer. She looked at them for a moment as she considered her plan for one last time. She took the syringe from the plastic wrapper, filled the syringe with the cleaning agent and injected a small amount into the cartons through the aluminium foil covered straw holes. When she had done, she put the syringe wrapper in her dressing gown pocket, put the cleaning agent in the sink cupboard, with the syringe wrapped in kitchen roll, and put the cartons in the refrigerator.

*

For several days, Damian had travelled between Eliza, at the Caplin residence, and Melanie, at her hair salon in Beechwood.

He had hovered beside Eliza in one of his many guises: invisibility. He was there to ensure she followed his wishes. He told her what to do, and think, and made her believe the voices she heard were inside her head. She was a compliant instrument, to do with as he pleased, and she never resisted. At last, he felt his efforts had been recognised and although he had tired, he would not stop until his mission was complete; Lisa's time in that dimension had to end, and Eliza would be his reward.

*

Eliza had agreed to help Mrs Caplin with a task before she left that day. With the door closed behind them, they checked around the garden and made their way towards Harry's shed.

Eliza opened the shed door, stepped inside, and pulled on the cord beside the door. A lightbulb lit dimly overhead. It came as no surprise to discover the shed was meticulous with not even a cobweb.

Garden tools hung from individual hooks on one wall. She imagined what it might feel like to stab someone through the heart with the shears and cut off their head with the hedge trimmer. She shuddered. Why did she have such thoughts?

Elizabeth followed. Without her glasses or contact lenses, she struggled to see the words on the boxes stacked on wooden shelving against another wall. She was in awe of how much stuff you needed to keep a garden maintained. As she looked up at the top shelf, she had not noticed the two-tread step ladder and walked into it. With one hand on the shelving, she reached down and massaged her shin. The shelving wobbled. A torch fell from the top shelf and narrowly missed her head. For a moment, she did not dare to move. She had expected someone to call out.

Eliza kept still too.

Elizabeth slowly moved her hand from the shelving and picked up the torch from the floor. The torch was still intact, but rattled when she shook it. She turned it on. A beam of light shone on to several five litre white plastic bottles on the top shelf.

With her foot, Eliza nudged the ladder forward, climbed up to the top rung, reached up and grabbed one of the bottles. There were no markings or hazard symbols on it. She put the bottle back and looked at the others beside it. There were different coloured liquids in each, of various levels; none were labelled. She decided not to open any of them to smell their contents.

She clambered down the ladder. Empty handed, she made her way out of the shed and waited outside, beside the door. She wondered what Mrs Caplin had wanted with hazardous liquid as she stared at her feet. She looked to her left and then to her right as though she expected to see someone.

Elizabeth became wary. She turned off the light, stepped outside and locked the door behind her. Had Eliza suspected anything? The hazardous liquid had been a backup plan in case the cleaning agent did not work.

Neither of them said a word, anxious they might be overheard, as they strolled back up towards the door.

A sudden movement in the window, of the bedroom Lisa and Peter stayed in, caught Elizabeth's attention, but when she looked up there was nothing to see. Was it a trick of the light or had someone hidden away?

Chapter Fifteen

The Discovery

Low clouds obscured the rising sun the day after the funeral.

Peter had slept upstairs while the weary grown-ups had paced the living room floor of Mr and Mrs Smyth's house. They took turns to look out of the window and watched as the fire ravaged Elizabeth's home.

Peter awoke. Disorientated, he checked around the bedroom for Mummy. He jumped out of bed and ran down the stairs. 'Where's Mummy?' He rubbed his eyes.

No one knew the answer. She had not returned, and no one had looked for her. Had they presumed that she had perished in the fire or drowned in the lake? They all smiled pitifully at him.

He did not ask again because he had his suspicions. He had sensed something bad would happen the day before.

Elizabeth crouched and held him tight.

Side by side, they all looked out of the window at the smoky orange glow. No one ate breakfast; no one was hungry. It was time they left. But would they have been able to get close enough to check on the devastation? And if they had, it was doubtful there would have been anything left to salvage.

Mr and Mrs Smyth stood in their garden. She stared across the lake at what was once a magnificent house. Tears filled her eyes. She put her hand over her mouth. Her stooped shoulders quivered. He wrapped his arm around her and pulled her closer. They watched as Elizabeth, Peter and Harry made their way towards *Diane*.

Harry focused the binoculars on what was once the Caplin residence. The house and all the outbuildings had gone. Mr Caplin's car was a burnt-out shell. The willow had blackened. He caught sight of Lisa's raft beside the island in the middle of the lake; it was caught in a bush. He started the engine and steered towards it.

'Might be best if Peter doesn't look,' he said as *Diane* drew closer to the raft.

'I'm a big boy now.' Peter tried to resist Elizabeth's attempts to turn his head away.

At first, the raft seemed empty, but Harry was the first to see Lisa's corpse in a pool of bodily fluids. Her glazed-over eyes appeared to stare up at the sky. Vomit trickled from the corners of her mouth.

Peter's eyes widened as he stared at his mother. He did not cry, focused his abilities and tried to bring her back to life. After a couple of minutes, when nothing had happened, he knew he had failed. She had been dead for too long. He lowered his head. A tear trickled down his cheek.

Elizabeth tried to console him. The small black shadows surrounded them.

*

The van, with two officers inside, was the first to be discovered and documented as an accident.

Divers recovered dead bodies from the lake. None were identified as who they had set out to look for; although, each was a person of interest.

Two bodies were recovered from the debris of one of the outbuildings. Forensic pathologists confirmed they were the remains of Robert Caplin and Melanie Willis.

Harry was right; it was Mr Caplin's car that had exploded and killed every firefighter at the scene.

The station was at a loss as to what had happened to the second fire engine as it had disappeared, along with every firefighter, without a trace.

*

Elizabeth was invited to the police station for a friendly chat. She remembered Robert had mentioned something once, while they had watched some drama on the television, about only giving brief answers or the police would try to pin a crime on you. She followed his advice.

Every part the grieving widow, she explained he had returned home without her knowledge. She had not noticed his car or had any idea why he was in the outbuilding. They had led separate lives. It was true when she said she had no idea as to why Melanie had been in there as well.

Although their bodies had been found at opposite ends of the outbuilding, the police still chose their words carefully as they asked if it was possible the two of them might have been in there together, for whatever reason.

Aware the two of them had never met, Elizabeth said it could have been possible, but it was doubtful.

Her mind wandered as the police continued to question her. *What's happened to Eliza? And how strange no one has asked after her or come looking for her.*

Eventually, the police had to let her go as they found no evidence to link her to anything that had happened.

*

When Damian had learnt of Susan's death, he saw his opportunity and visited Melanie in her hair salon. They met later that day for a coffee. He explained how imperative it was she go with him to the Caplin Residence. If she did not, Victoria would spend an eternity in purgatory and there would be no escape for her. But he could set her free and reunite them. However, he did not have such power.

Melanie had not seen Victoria in the flames. The vision had been another demon who imitated humans.

*

Harry's postman noticed the previous day's post had not been removed from his letterbox. He heard the television blaring as he tried to push the post through, but the basket, on the other side of the door, was already full. With a gardening magazine still to deliver, he knocked, stood back, and waited.

There was no answer or any sounds from a rattling key in the keyhole or from a latch. Perhaps Harry had been unable to hear over the din of the western movie he watched.

The postman knocked again, harder, and when there was still no answer, he crouched and shouted through the letterbox. An ice-cold breeze wrapped around his face.

Harry's neighbour stepped out on to the corridor with bare feet. He wore faded striped pyjama bottoms and a white T-shirt; neither appeared to have seen the inside of a washing machine for weeks, if ever. He leant against his door frame and watched as the postman, who was still crouched and held on to the letterbox flap, remained still. 'I think there must be something wrong with the old boy. His telly's been on for days. It's unusual for him. Don't usually hear him,' he said. He lifted his T-shirt and wiggled his finger inside his navel. 'I'll give the police a call.' He turned round, scratched his backside and went back inside.

The postman, who had moved away from the letterbox, and the neighbour, who had put on a cardigan, waited until the police arrived.

The police knocked on Harry's door. When there was no answer, they tried the handle. The door was unlocked. They found him seated upright in his well-worn armchair. He was dead.

An autopsy confirmed he had died from natural causes.

He had always said once you stopped working, you might as well give up on life.

Chapter Sixteen

The Crematorium

Elizabeth had written a suicide note, on Lisa's behalf, explaining how she could no longer live with herself after everything she had done, although no specific details were given. She used a typewriter, so whoever found it would not be able to compare handwriting styles, and then she disposed of the ribbon. She left it unsigned. She had put the note in Lisa's jacket pocket before she got into the raft. Lisa had not known it was there.

*

An obituary, in the local newspapers of Beechwood and the Lake District, stated where and when Lisa's cremation would take place; a non-religious service with a few words spoken by a stranger.

Elizabeth did not deliver a eulogy and had not tried to prepare one. Not because she could not think of what to say or because she was intoxicated. It was because she had Peter to think about. What if she had accidentally said something about how Lisa had died?

No favourite song or music played as she had not known of Lisa's taste; however, several whispered conversations interrupted the silence.

The service chapel at the crematorium was crowded. Some of the mourners leant against the back wall and down the sides of the room. Most – who were already dead themselves – displayed varying levels of transparency and distanced themselves to avoid occupying the same space.

The demon was seated, cross-legged, on top of the closed coffin. Although human in shape, it looked neither male nor female. It was pale in colour: a translucent white. It had no ears, nose, or mouth, and had two grey sockets instead of eyes. A framed school photograph of Lisa, when she was about eleven years old with a wonky fringe and a patch of acne on her chin, was displayed in front of the demon.

The demon was not there to cause any further torment, despite it knowing the truth about what Elizabeth had done. It was there, out of curiosity, to check on that lifetime's achievements. It also needed to double-check who the other demons were; something that was inconclusive until after death. Only other demons would be able to see it in its true form.

The spirits, in front of it, were liberated; the black shadow no longer able to hold them captive.

Damian and Melanie's plan was put into action before their final trip to Elizabeth's home; the sycamore in Beechwood had been felled and its roots poisoned while the black shadows were preoccupied.

Looking around the room, the demon recalled how each of the spirits were taken, their injuries still evident. It also knew the details of how each of the living inside the chapel would die, and when.

The ceiling and wall lights flickered. That number of souls in one room drained the electricity supply, and not only in that building; lights within a mile radius flashed intermittently while neighbouring homeowners cursed their electricity providers.

Elizabeth was on the front row with her arm around Peter's shoulders. She kept squeezing his right shoulder as she stared across at Lisa's photograph and what was behind it, seated on the coffin. She had found the photograph in her handbag and wondered how it had got there. Mrs Smyth had supplied the frame. All other family photographs were destroyed in the fire.

Peter cuddled up to Elizabeth. Was he aware of what his grandmother had done to his mother? He stared at the floor. Occasionally, he wiped tears on his sleeve and looked at what was seated on the coffin.

One of the small black shadows hovered close-by; the chosen one, destined to be his guardian for the rest of his days.

Karl was seated beside Peter. He put on a brave face for the sake of his two daughters. Neither of the girls had spoken since arriving. They found it hard to understand how they had lost both their mother and their auntie in such a short time.

Behind Elizabeth, seated on the edge of her seat, Grandma Buckley leant forward and rested her hand on Elizabeth's shoulder. Advised by the family doctor not to travel, Grandad Buckley convalesced at home after a long bout of flu. Grandma seemed unaware he kept appearing beside her, albeit a translucent version.

The souls of Fred and Katherine hovered on the same row. She had vomit down her chin and on her clothes from where she had overdosed on that fateful day.

Grandma and Grandad Parkins were absent. They had claimed the slow-moving traffic on the M6 would have prevented them from getting there on time and to avoid any embarrassment, they had decided to turn round and go home.

On the opposite side, on the front row, hovered Harry's soul. Unaware of his own passing, he kept turning round and looking at the double doors; hopeful that Eliza might make an entrance. No one had seen or heard from her since that night at Mr and Mrs Smyth's house.

Michelle Shaw, Lisa's previous housemate, was seated beside him. She looked well; the prescription drugs helped. It was her mother who had noticed the announcement in the obituary section of The Beechwood Chronicle. As Michelle had made the journey by train and taxi that morning, she looked out at the passing countryside and regretted they had not stayed in touch.

More familiar faces were seated behind them. Shocked to hear of Lisa's death, Barry and June Hayes had left Sally to run Woodhayes Bed and Breakfast, for the day, to allow them to say their goodbyes. Lisa had thought highly of the couple, all the years she had worked for them, as they treated her like a daughter.

Adam and Rob, from the walking group Lisa used to attend, were seated beside them. The group no longer ran because most of the members had passed away within several months of each other. Derek, who had been reunited with his late wife Emma, Mavis, Mr Kenneth and Mrs Irene Butterworth, were present in spirit form and hovered at the back of the room; each unscathed after they had died peacefully in their sleep.

The demon looked across at Jack Lowe's pitiful spirit at the far end of that row. It remembered the mugging and the fear and humiliation that went with it. It felt instant gratification when it noticed his torso sliced open and his intestines draped over his legs like a throw.

Behind Grandma Buckley were the spirits of George and Melanie with their daughter, Victoria, between them. He had bruises around his neck where he had supposedly hung himself in Beechwood Park years earlier. Melanie's skin shone bright red with adjoining blisters. Victoria's tattered red dress still dripped, but the drops evaporated before they hit the floor. Despite their gruesome deaths, their smiles revealed a peacefulness as if the previous years of hardship and loneliness had never happened.

Beside them were Ben and an expectant Amanda Cooper. He gazed at her admiringly. Both were oblivious that they had passed away or that they would never get to meet their unborn child. Neither of them questioned why they attended the funeral service of someone they did not know.

The spirit of Mrs Blake, who was no longer a gossip, hovered on the end of the row; her right hip still overhung the side of her chair.

Beside her, Martyn's spirit was no longer forced to endure an addictive nature. He hovered, as if still seated in his wheelchair, and blocked the aisle. Whenever the living walked through him, they experienced a tingling sensation.

On the opposite row, behind Barry and June Hayes, hovered Elizabeth's late husbands. Severely burnt Robert had bullet holes in his head and chest. John kept screwing up his face while he gripped his arm and chest.

Beside them hovered the spirits of Daniel Wood – the chancer who took his flirting too far – with a messy exit wound at the back of his head, and Steven Brook, Lisa's late husband, drenched after his fall from the bridge. He scratched his groin, but to no avail.

Beside them was Linda Hays's spirit. She had retrieved her head from the river, after Lisa had booted it over the treetops, and tried to hold it in place on her neck.

Derrick Mole's spirit did the same while his wife's spirit, Sylvia, nursed the spider bite on her neck that dripped bloodied pus.

Larry Hennessy's spirit looked dazed; his head was split wide open after Derrick had walloped it with an axe. June Pennock's spirit brain continued to be gnawed by hundreds of insects; however, they could not burrow any deeper.

Beside Michelle hovered the spirits of Susan and Bill. A whiff of fuel went with their severe burns. Susan appeared oblivious to her family being in the same room and that they were filled with grief over her passing.

A spirit, dressed in walking gear, kept looking over his shoulders as he searched for his misplaced rucksack.

Beside him, in spirit – a previous neighbour – Josh danced with a grin on his face as if surrounded by family and friends.

There were several faces, in and amongst, that the demon did not recognise. Maybe they were people who enjoyed funerals or had attended the wrong service. Wait, it did recognise one of the faces: Lisa's old games teacher, Miss Aitken. She stared directly at it.

A coach load of spirits arrived: a bride and groom with their guests. They hovered, in and amongst, in search of a space.

The spirit of Lisa's real father, Peter Hurst, was present. The smell of cigar smoke surrounded him. He watched the demon and smiled.

The doors at the back of the chapel closed gently and yet the sound echoed as if the room was empty and vast. Everyone fell silent and looked forward.

The demon ascended and hovered over the coffin. It made its way around the room. It started with the dead and writhed in front of them as though it tried to distract them.

Most of the spirits could not see the demon.

The demon made its way around the room again and got closer to the living. It liked how they smelt: fresh or salty and ready for the taking. It had to remind itself, however, that it was there only as an observer.

The living, who had sensed the demon's presence, leant back on their seats.

A decrepit man entered the chapel from a side door and made his way to the front of the room. A neat thin line of silver hair started behind one ear, went around the back of his head, and finished behind his other ear.

With mannerisms like Damian's, the demon wondered if it might be him in another guise. The demon hovered beside the man and inspected him closer, but noticed his smell was different: an odour from the living world.

The demon became bored. It left the chapel in search of the furnace that would incinerate the body.

It found the furnace in a dark cold room. Its open door was an invitation for it to enter. It accepted, huddled in a corner, and waited.

A little later, the coffin rolled in. The framed photograph was laid on the lid, picture up. The furnace's blackened door closed. The flames rose and engulfed the coffin.

Chapter Seventeen

The End

Curious to know if anyone would collect Lisa's ashes, the demon waited in the chapel and watched as the spirits conversed. Many services and several days later, the remaining spirits turned into orbs and left.

Elizabeth and Peter arrived in a taxi early one morning to collect the urn. It was an overcast day that mirrored their moods.

Careful not to spill the ashes on the back seat, as they made their way back to Mr and Mrs Smyth's house, she held the urn between her thighs. The journey was quiet.

The urn was placed beside Peter's bed, so he could say goodnight before he went to sleep.

That same night, while he was asleep in bed, Elizabeth was in the kitchen with a mug of hot chocolate before she turned in for the night. Lisa's mobile phone started to ring. It was inside a polythene bag with the suicide note and other items that were found in Lisa's pockets when her body was recovered from the raft. She thought the battery would have gone flat. When she answered the mobile phone, she was surprised to hear an estate agent from Beechwood on the other end. He wanted to speak to Lisa about her plans to buy the old family home. Did she still want to go ahead because he had not heard from her or her solicitor? Elizabeth passed on the sad news and informed him that she was interested.

Several weeks later, Elizabeth and Peter moved back to Beechwood with the urn, a suitcase and a boxful of essentials they had bought while staying with Mr and Mrs Smyth. There would be plenty of money in the bank to buy whatever they needed for their new home with the proceeds from *Diane*, Lisa's savings and life insurance, Robert's life insurance, from the sale of The Red Squirrel, the hotel, and the Caplin residence once it was renovated to its former glory.

After a couple of hours of exploring his new home, Peter picked up the urn and made his way towards the door. 'Park, Grandma,' he said adamantly.

Elizabeth nodded. It seemed a suitable place to spread Lisa's ashes. Fearful he might fall, she took the urn from him, and they made their way towards the park.

She put the urn on the ground, beside the swing, and helped him climb on. She pushed him gently and reflected: *I wonder what Lisa got up to when she came down here.* She stepped back and looked around. *Where would be the best place to scatter her ashes? In the river, under the waterfall, perhaps?* She remembered that was where Victoria's body was found, and she shook her head.

Realising he had gone unheard, he stopped pleading for her to push him higher. As if he could read her mind, he pointed towards where the sycamore had once stood.

She nodded and then gawped. What had happened to the sycamore with the pentangle? There was not even a stump or any protruding roots. It was like the tree had never been there.

He jumped off the swing, landed on his feet and quickly moved out of its way.

Before he had chance to pick up the urn, she grabbed it. It was too big for him to carry. What would have happened if he had tripped or dropped it?

He narrowed his eyes as they made their way towards where the sycamore had stood. They stopped a few feet away. She gestured for him to wait, moved closer, put the urn down, and stepped back again. 'Would you like to do it?' she said.

'Together.'

She edged forward and took the lid off the urn; it was a tight fit. He watched but did not move. With the lid still in her hand, she left the urn and stepped back again.

It took a moment longer before he picked up the courage to move. They held hands, moved towards the urn, and peered inside.

He found it hard to believe that was all that remained of his mother. His bottom lip quivered, and his tears flowed, but he made no sound.

The demon, which was once Lisa, appeared behind them. Disorientated, it looked around and at where the sycamore used to be. It leant forward to get one last look at Peter and then vanished.

Elizabeth and Peter crouched. She placed her left hand on the left side of the urn. He placed his right hand on the right side. They slowly tipped the urn forward. The ashes fell towards the ground. Where the air had been still moments earlier, a gentle breeze blew. They straightened up. She grabbed his hand. They stepped back and watched as Lisa's ashes swirled above the ground.

The breeze calmed. The ashes settled where the sycamore had been.

She looked at her watch but did not take in the time. 'Sorry, Peter, we need to get back.' A gardener was expected at the house that afternoon. The previous owners had not sorted out the back garden. She was undecided if the garden should be turfed or concreted.

They made their way along the path. He stopped, turned round, and said, 'Bye, Mummy.' He waved as if he could still see her, turned round and ran to catch up with his grandmother.

A group of teenagers walked towards them: three boys and a girl. One of the boys carried a holdall on his shoulder, which he struggled to carry. The girl had a boardgame under her arm with the word Ouija on its lid.

Elizabeth shuffled Peter in front of her. She needed to watch him as the serious-looking teenagers walked by, but they paid no heed.

'You can visit Mummy whenever you want. Just let me know if you need to.'

He nodded.

They left Beechwood Park and walked over the bridge.

*

The boy put the holdall on the ground beside where the sycamore used to be, unzipped it, got out four mats and passed one to each of his friends. They unrolled them, put them at their feet and ensured they were flat. Next out of the holdall was a statue. He placed it on the ground in front of them. They knelt on their mats, stretched their arms above their heads, and as they leant forward, a tree sprout sprung through the ground.